"She's beautiful," Russ whispered.

He lightly touched Emily's hand and the baby closed her fingers over his thumb. "Just like a tiny angel."

There was so much emotion in his voice. Was this the same man who had stared down gunmen in the alley?

Julia had come to this small Texas town to find Emily's father—and had also found the man of her dreams.

Well, almost.

Russ was rough around the edges and perhaps a little dangerous, but he had a way of making her remember that she was alive. The energy between them was electric…and was even more special because Emily was there.

DELORES FOSSEN

DADDY DEVASTATING

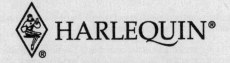

TORONTO • NEW YORK • LONDON
AMSTERDAM • PARIS • SYDNEY • HAMBURG
STOCKHOLM • ATHENS • TOKYO • MILAN • MADRID
PRAGUE • WARSAW • BUDAPEST • AUCKLAND

Recycling programs
for this product may
not exist in your area.

ISBN-13: 978-0-373-69478-5

DADDY DEVASTATING

Copyright © 2010 by Delores Fossen

ABOUT THE AUTHOR

Imagine a family tree that includes Texas cowboys, Choctaw and Cherokee Indians, a Louisiana pirate and a Scottish rebel who battled side by side with William Wallace. With ancestors like that, it's easy to understand why Texas author and former air force captain Delores Fossen feels as if she were genetically predisposed to writing romances. Along the way to fulfilling her DNA destiny, Delores married an air force top gun who just happens to be of Viking descent. With all those romantic bases covered, she doesn't have to look too far for inspiration.

Books by Delores Fossen

HARLEQUIN INTRIGUE

*Texas Paternity
†Texas Paternity: Boots and Booties
††Texas Maternity: Hostages
**Five-Alarm Babies

CAST OF CHARACTERS

Special Agent Russ Gentry—He's a rough-around-the-edges FBI agent in the middle of bringing down a notorious black-market baby dealer. But his investigation becomes even more dangerous when drop-dead-gorgeous Texas heiress Julia Howell arrives in a seedy border town to tell him he's the daddy of a newborn baby girl.

Julia Howell—She made a promise to her dying cousin that she would find her newborn niece's father, but Julia hadn't counted on a daddy mix-up. Nor had the guarded heiress even thought she could get past her old wounds and fears and fall for the likes of bad boy Russ Gentry.

Emily—She's only two weeks old and too young to understand that she's surrounded by danger. Luckily she also has Russ and Julia, two people who already love her more than life itself.

Milo Dawson—The key to bringing down a baby broker and recovering a stolen child, but neither Russ nor the FBI trust him.

Silas Durant—Russ's fellow FBI agent and partner. Is he a dirty agent, or is someone setting him up?

Aaron Richardson—His stolen son is at the heart of Russ's investigation, but Aaron's past indiscretions might come back to haunt him.

Tracy Richardson—Aaron's wife and the mother of the stolen child. Unlike her cool and reserved husband, her temper and impulsive behavior could get in the way of the investigation.

Sylvia Hartman—Milo's assistant who could have her own agenda when it comes to Russ, Julia and the stolen child.

Chapter One

San Saba, Texas

Russ Gentry cursed under his breath when the brunette stepped through the doors of the Silver Dollar bar.

Hell.

She'd followed him.

He had spotted her about fifteen minutes earlier on the walk from his hotel to the bar. She had trailed along behind him in her car, inching up the street, as if he were too stupid or blind to notice her or her sleek silver Jaguar. He had decided to ignore her for the time being anyway, because he'd hoped she was lost.

Obviously not.

Now, he had two questions—who was she? And was this about to turn even more dangerous than it already was?

He watched her from over the top of the bottle of Lone Star beer that the bartender had just served him. She was tall—five-nine, or better—and she was clutching a key ring that had a small can of pepper spray hooked onto it. There was a thin, gold-colored purse tucked beneath her arm, but it didn't have any telltale bulges of a weapon, and her snug blue dress skimmed over her curvy body, so that carrying concealed would have been next to impossible.

Heck, in that dress concealing a paper-thin nicotine patch would have been a challenge. It was a garment obviously meant to keep her cool on a scalding-hot Texas day.

It did the opposite of making him cool.

Under different circumstances, Russ might have taken the time to savor the view, and he might have even made an attempt to hit on her.

But this wasn't different circumstances.

He'd learned the hard way that even a momentary lapse of concentration could have deadly results. As a reminder of that, he rubbed his fingers over the scar just to the left of his heart. The reminder, however, didn't help when the woman made eye contact.

With Willie Nelson blaring from the jukebox, she wended her way through the customers seated at the mismatched tables scattered around the room. The neon sign on the wall that advertised tequila flashed an assortment of tawdry colors over her.

Without taking her gaze from him, she stopped only a few inches away. Close enough for Russ to catch her scent. She smelled high priced and looked high maintenance.

"We need to talk," she said, and slid onto the barstool next to him, her silky dress whispering against the leather seat.

Oh, man. Keeping her here would hardly encourage his informant to make contact. Hell, the only thing her presence would do was create problems for him.

"I'm not interested, darlin'," Russ grumbled, hoping that his surly attitude would cause her to leave.

It didn't.

"Well, I'm interested in you," she said, her voice much louder than Willie's.

In fact, she was loud enough to attract the few customers who hadn't already noticed her when she walked in. Of course, with her sex-against-the-bathroom-wall body, Russ figured she'd likely caught the attention of every one of the male patrons.

He eased his beer down onto the bar and turned slightly, so he could look her in the eyes. "Back off," he warned, under his breath.

"I can't."

Okay. He hadn't expected her to say that or ignore his warning.

Her clothes, the sleek sable-colored hair that tumbled onto her shoulders and even her tone might have screamed that she was confident about what she was doing, or about to do, but just beneath those ice-blue eyes was deeply rooted concern. And fear.

That put Russ on full alert.

"Look," he whispered. "This is no place for you. Leave."

She huffed and took the purse from beneath her arm. When she reached inside, Russ caught onto her hand. And got an uneasy thought.

"You can't be Milo," he mumbled. Because from what he'd been told about the would-be contact, Milo was a forty-something-year-old male. Of course, his source could have been wrong.

She stiffened slightly, looked more than a little confused, but it lasted just seconds, before she pushed off his grip. "I'm Julia Howell."

The name sounded vaguely familiar, but he couldn't

press her for more information. If she was Milo, or
Milo's replacement, Russ would find out soon enough.
And then he could get this show started. But he didn't
like the bad feeling that was settling in his gut.

She placed her purse next to his beer, but held on
to the pepper-spray keychain. "You didn't introduce
yourself, but I know you're Russell James Gentry."

Hell.

Russ looked around to make sure no one had heard
her use his real name. It was possible. The body-builder
bartender seemed to be trying a little too hard not to
look their way. Ditto for the middle-aged guy near the
door. And the dark haired man in the corner. Unlike the
bartender and the one by the door, Russ was positive
this dark haired guy had been following him for days,
and Russ had let him keep on following him because
he had wanted to send Milo a message—that he had
nothing to hide.

Which was a lie, of course.

Russ had plenty to hide.

"You're mistaken," Russ insisted. "I'm Jimmy
Marquez."

"I'm not mistaken." She obviously wasn't picking up
on any of his nonverbal cues to stay quiet. "I have proof
you're Russell James Gentry," she said, and reached for
her purse again.

He didn't have any idea what she had in that gold
bag to prove his identity, and he didn't really care. He
had to do something to get her to turn tail and run.

Russ swiveled his bar stool toward her, and in the
same motion he slapped his left palm on her thigh. This
would get her out of there in record time. He snared
her gaze and tried to give her one hell of a nonverbal

warning before he ran his hand straight up to her silk panties.

No, make that lace.

But she still didn't run. She gasped, her eyes narrowed and she drew back her perfectly manicured hand, no doubt ready to slap him into the middle of next week. And she would have, too, if Russ hadn't snagged her wrist.

When she tried to use her other hand to slug him, he had to give up the panty ploy so he could restrain her.

Russ put his mouth right against her ear. "We're leaving now. Get up."

Because her mouth was on his cheek, he felt the word "no" start to form on her peach-tinged lips. Judging from the way the muscles tightened in her arms and legs, she was gearing up for an all-out fight with him.

Gutsy.

But stupid.

He was a good six inches taller than she was, and he had her by at least seventy pounds. Still, he preferred not to have to wrestle her out of there, but he would if it meant saving her lace-pantied butt.

"If you know what's good for you," Russ whispered to her, "you'll do as I say. Or else you can die right here. Your choice, lady."

But he didn't give her a choice. He couldn't. Russ shoved the purse back under her arm, grabbed the pepper-spray keychain and used brute force to wrench her off the barstool. He started in the direction of the door.

Their sudden exit drew some attention, especially from the bartender and the bald guy, but no one made a move to interfere. Thankfully, the bar wasn't the kind of place where people thought about doing their civic duty and assisting a possible damsel in distress.

Julia Howell squirmed and struggled all the way to the door. "I won't let you hurt me," she spat out. "I won't ever let anyone hurt me again."

That sounded like the voice of old baggage, but Russ wasn't interested.

He got her outside, finally. It was dusk, still way too hot for early September, and the sidewalks weren't exactly empty. No cops, but there were two "working girls" making their way past the bar. They stopped and stared, but Russ shot them a *back-off* glare. He was good at glares, too, and he wasn't surprised when the women scurried away, their stilettos tapping against the concrete.

"How did you know my name?" Russ asked. "What so-called proof do you have?"

He didn't look directly at Julia Howell. Too risky. He kept watch all around them. And he shoved her into the narrow, dark alley that separated the bar from a transmission repair shop that had already closed for the day. He moved away from the sidewalk, about twenty feet, until he was in the dark of the alley.

"I won't let you hurt me," she repeated, and tried to knee him in the groin. She missed. Her rock-hard kneecap slammed into his thigh instead, and had him seeing stars and cursing a blue streak.

Tired of the fight and the lack of answers to his simple questions, Russ put her against the brick wall. He wasn't gentle, either, and he used his body to hold her in place. "Tell me how you know my name."

Julia didn't stop struggling, and she continued to ram herself into him. It only took her a few moments to realize that that wasn't a good idea—her breasts thrusting against his chest. Her sex pounding in the general vicinity of his.

She groaned in frustration and dropped the back of her head against the wall. Her breathing also revved up. And now that the fight had apparently gone out of her, the panic was starting to set in. Her chest began to pump as if starved for air, and he could see the pulse hammer in her throat. Sweat popped out above her upper lip.

"Calm down," he warned. "You can't answer my questions if you're hyperventilating."

That earned him a glare, and like him, she was good at them, too. It took her a moment to get her breathing under control so she could speak. "I used facial-recognition software to learn who you are."

"Excuse me?"

"I found you through facial-recognition software," she repeated, through gusts of breath. "I know you're Russell James Gentry."

Russ stared at her, trying to make sense of this, but her explanation wasn't helping much. He shifted her keys in his hand so he could grab her purse. There wasn't much room in the bag, and it was crammed with photos and a cell phone, but he quickly spotted what he was looking for.

Her driver's license.

It was there tucked behind a clear sleeve attached to the inside of the bag. The name and photo matched what she'd told him, but Russ wasn't about to take any chances.

While keeping her restrained, he shoved her purse back under her arm and took out his cell from his front jeans pocket. He pressed the first name in his list of contacts, and as expected, Silas Duran answered on the first ring.

Russ didn't say the man's name aloud, nor his own, and he didn't even offer a greeting. He wanted this done quickly and hoped it would be. Silas was a new partner. A replacement. And Russ wasn't sure how good Silas would be when thrown a monkey wrench.

Like now.

"Julia Elise Howell," Russ stated. "Run a quick check on her."

He immediately heard Silas making clicks on a keyboard. He waited, with Julia staring holes in him and with her breath gusting. He wouldn't be able to contain her for long. Well, he could physically, but that wouldn't be a smart thing to do in public. Someone might eventually call the cops.

"She's a San Antonio heiress who manages a charity foundation," Silas said. "Her father was a well-known real-estate developer. Both parents are dead. She's single. Twenty-nine. Says here she's considered a recluse, and that makes sense, because the only pictures that popped up were ones from over a decade ago. She's worth about fifty million. Why?"

None of that info explained why she had walked into the bar and plopped down next to him. "She's here. In San Saba. About an inch away from my face."

"Why?" Silas repeated. "Is she connected to the meeting with Milo?"

"I'm about to ask the same thing. She has a cell phone in her purse, probably in her own name. Check and make sure this really is Julia Howell in front of me."

A minute or so passed before Silas said, "She's there.

Well, her phone is anyway. Should I send someone to take care of her?"

"Not yet." Russ slapped his cell shut and crammed it back into his pocket.

Well, at least Julia was who she said she was. That was something at least.

Maybe.

Russ stared at her. "Why and how exactly did you find me?" he asked. "Not the facial-recognition software. I got that part. I want to know how you made the match and why."

She tipped her head to her left breast, and it took him a moment to realize she was motioning toward her purse and not the body contact between them. "Your picture is in there. A friend owns a security company, and he fed your photo through the software and came up with a match."

"Impossible." His records were buried under layers and layers of false information. Of course, his face wasn't buried. But any info about him was.

"Not impossible. My friend is very good at what he does, and he had access to security cameras all over the state. He ran the facial-recognition software twenty-four/seven, until he finally spotted you at a bank in San Antonio. Then he asked around, offered money." She hesitantly added, "And one of the bank employees gave us your name."

Russ wanted to punch the brick wall. He'd covered all bases, or so he thought. Yes, he had gone to the San Antonio bank to take care of some family business, but he hadn't counted on a chatty employee ratting him out. Nor had he counted on anyone digging this deep to find him.

"Even after we had your name, we couldn't find out anything about you," she continued. "Finally, one of the P.I.s who works for my friend spotted your face on a traffic-camera feed and was able to do the match. That's how I knew you were in San Saba. The P.I. came down here, followed you for several days and found out where you were staying."

That was a P.I.? Russ had thought it was one of Milo's men following him and checking him out. That's why he hadn't done anything about the tail. Mercy. And now that mistake had come back to bite him in the butt.

"The P.I. wanted to approach you, but I thought it best if I did it myself," she added. "Because it is such a personal matter."

Her explanation prompted more profanity and a dozen more questions, but Russ started with a simple one. "Why go through the trouble to look for me?"

"Because of Lissa," she said, as if the answer were obvious. "Lissa gave me your photograph."

Russ was sure he looked as pole-axed as he felt. "Who the hell is Lissa?"

For the first time since they'd started this little wrestling match and confusing conversation, Julia relaxed. At least, she went limp, as if she'd huffed all the breath right out of her. "My first cousin, Lissa McIntyre." Then her eyes narrowed. "Are you saying you don't remember her?"

"Yeah, that's exactly what I'm saying," Russ answered, honestly.

Her muscles went stiff again, and the remainder of the fear faded from her expression. It was replaced by a healthy dose of anger. "Let me refresh your memory. San Antonio. Last December. You met Lissa at a downtown bar, and after a night of drinking you went into one of those photo booths on the Riverwalk and had your picture taken."

Russ went through the past months. Yeah, it was possible he'd met a woman in a bar. But he certainly didn't remember anybody named Lissa, and he absolutely didn't remember taking a picture in a photo booth.

"Why are you here?" he asked, pressing her further.

"Because Lissa wanted me to find you." Julia took a deep breath. "She's dead. She was injured in the hostage standoff at the San Antonio Maternity Hospital two weeks ago. The doctors tried to save her but couldn't." Her voice broke, and tears sprang into her blue eyes. "She used her dying breath to ask me to find you."

He'd heard about the hostage situation, of course, it'd been all over the news. And he was also aware there'd been several deaths. But that had nothing to do with him.

"I'm sorry for your loss," Russ said, because he didn't know what else to say. This still wasn't making any sense. "But why the hell would your cousin want you to find me?"

She stared at him. "You don't remember?"

"Remember what?"

There was some movement at the back end of the alley. A shadow maybe. Maybe something worse. So Russ eased his hand into the slide holster in the back waistband of his jeans.

She snatched the purse from beneath her arm and practically ripped the bag open. "Look, I know Lissa was probably a one-night stand, but you have to remember her."

Julia pulled out a photo of an attractive brunette and practically stuck it in his face. Russ glanced at it, just a glance, and he turned his attention back to that damn shadow.

Was it Milo?

Or had one of the working girls grown a conscience and called the cops?

Those were the best-case scenarios. But Russ had a feeling this wasn't a best-case scenario kind of moment. He took out his gun and kept it behind his back.

"Well?" Julia demanded. If she noticed the gun, she didn't have a reaction—which meant she almost certainly hadn't seen it. "Do you remember Lissa?"

That was an easy answer. "No. Why should I?"

She made a sound, not of anger but outrage, and grabbed another photo from her purse. Russ glanced at it, too, and saw the baby. A newborn, swaddled in a pink blanket.

He froze.

Oh, this was suddenly getting a lot clearer. Or was it? Was this hot brunette really a black-market baby seller? If so, she certainly didn't look the part.

"Did Milo send you?" he snarled. "Is this the kid the seller's offering? Because it's not supposed to be a girl."

Julia went still again. Very still. And Russ risked looking at her so he could see what was going on in her eyes.

"Seller?" she repeated. There was a lot of emotion in that one word. Confusion, fear and a boatload of concern. "No. The newborn in the picture is Lissa's."

"I don't understand." Was she trying to sell her own cousin's kid?

"Well, you *should* understand, because you're the baby's father."

What?! It felt as if someone had slugged him in the gut. "Father?" Russ managed to say, though it didn't have any sound to it.

Ah, hell.

Russ's stomach dropped to the cracked dirty concrete, but that was the only reaction he managed. There certainly wasn't time to question Julia about what she'd just said about him being a father.

The movement at the back of the alley grabbed his full attention. Because the shadow moved.

So did Russ.

He shoved the photos back into her purse and gave Julia the keychain with the pepper spray. She might need it. He hooked his left arm around her, pushing her behind him.

"What's wrong?" she asked. Julia looked around, and no doubt saw the figure dressed in dark clothes and wearing a ski mask.

Russ took aim.

But it was too late.

Another man stepped into the alley from the front sidewalk. He lifted his gun. So did the ski mask wearing man.

They were trapped.

Chapter Two

Julia clamped her teeth over her bottom lip to choke back a scream. What was happening?

"Lower your gun," the man at the front of the alley warned Russell. "Keep your hands where I can see them and don't make any sudden moves."

The man giving the orders was tall and lanky and wore jeans and a scruffy t-shirt—unlike his comrade at the other end of the alley who wasn't wearing a ski mask. And that frightened Julia even more, because it meant Russell and she could identify him.

And that meant the man might kill them for that reason alone.

Of course, he might have already had killing on his mind before he stepped into that alley.

Julia cursed herself. How could she have gotten herself into this situation again? She didn't have the answer for that yet, but she wouldn't just stand around and whimper about this, and she wouldn't give up without a fight.

She cleared her throat so her voice would have some sound. "What's going on?" she asked Russell.

Not that she expected him to tell her. So far, he hadn't volunteered much, and she didn't trust him any further than she could throw him. Still, Russell had stepped in front of her when the men first appeared, and he appeared to be trying to protect her.

For all the good it'd do.

They literally had two guns aimed right at them.

Julia felt the jolt of panic and tried to get it under control before it snowballed. Not easy to do. Everything inside her was telling her to run for her life.

"Keep quiet," Russell growled. "Stay calm. And slow down your breathing." He glanced back at her, his coffee-brown eyes narrowed and intense. His gaze slashed from one end of the alley to the other, and he finally lifted his hands in surrender.

"Who are you?" Russell asked the man.

The ski-masked gunman stayed put, but the other one walked closer. He was dressed better than his partner. His crisp khakis and pale blue shirt made him look more like a preppy college professor than a criminal, and there were some threads of gray in his dark hair. But there was no doubt in Julia's mind that this man was up to no good.

"Who are *you?*" the preppy guy echoed, aiming his stare at Russell.

"Jimmy Marquez," Russell replied.

Julia hoped she didn't look surprised that he'd given them that name—the same one he'd used in the bar when she had first approached him. It wasn't his real name, she was sure of that. She'd paid Sentron Securities too much money for them to make a mistake like that.

"And who the hell are you?" Russell added, staring at the approaching man.

"Milo."

She felt the muscles in Russell's arm relax. Why, she didn't know.

"Well, it's about damn time you showed up," Russell snarled. "You should have been here yesterday. I waited in that bar half the night for you."

Milo offered no apology, no explanation. He merely lifted his shoulder and tipped his head to the ski-masked guy.

Both men lowered their weapons.

That didn't make Julia breathe any easier. Something dangerous and probably illegal was likely about to happen, and she had no idea if she could rely on Russell. Thankfully, he kept his gun gripped in his hand.

She held on to the pepper spray.

Lissa had been stupid, or duped, to get involved with a man like Russell Gentry. Julia should have ignored Lissa's deathbed request that she personally find the father of Lissa's child. There was no way Julia would hand over the baby to the likes of him, and it didn't matter that she would be violating Lissa's dying wish.

"Who's the woman?" Milo asked, staring holes into Julia.

As much as she distrusted Russell, Julia distrusted this one even more.

"Julia Howell," Russell said.

Mercy, he'd used her real name. Not that it would matter who she was to these men. But she preferred that criminals not know who she was.

"She's a *friend*," Russell added, "and she was just leaving." He nudged Julia in the direction of the front of the alley, and that was the only invitation Julia needed to get moving. She turned.

But didn't get far.

Milo stepped in front of her, calmly reached out and took her purse. Did he intend to rob her? Julia didn't care. She only wanted out of there. But he blocked her again when she tried to move.

"She's not carrying a weapon," Russell said.

But Milo didn't take his word for it. The man dug through her purse and pulled out the three pictures inside. He glanced at the first two, shoved them back inside, but the third picture he held up.

It was the one of Lissa's baby.

Julia could feel her pulse thicken and throb. The throbbing got worse, and she tried to snatch the photo from his hand. Milo held on and aimed his stony gaze at Russell.

"Is this one of the babies you've acquired?" Milo asked.

Julia started to speak up, to tell them that the child was her cousin's, but then she remembered something Russell had asked before the goons showed up.

"Is this the kid the seller's offering?"

Sweet heaven. What was going on here? Were these men involved with black-marketing babies? If so, they weren't going to get their hands on Emily. She would kill them before she let that happen.

"No. It's my kid," Russell said. "Julia came here to tell me that I'm a daddy. Fate can sure be a kick in the butt, huh?"

Milo volleyed glances between the photo and Russell. "This is your child?"

There was skepticism in his tone, but Julia figured Milo had to see the resemblance. Baby Emily had the shape of her daddy's mouth and his sandy brown hair. Of course, Emily looked sweet and innocent, whereas her father, well, he just looked dangerous. That'd been Julia's first impression of him anyway, and he wasn't doing anything to change that.

Russell turned, angling his body, so he could slip his arm around her waist. The corner of his mouth hitched into a cocky smile that only he and a rock star could have managed to pull off, and those dark brown eyes that'd been so intense just a second earlier, softened.

It was an act.

"Yeah, that's my kid," Russell said to Milo, but the fake smile was directed at her. "Julia and I have got some things to work out, but the old feelings are still there," he added, all slow and sexy.

Then he leaned in. Too close. Julia was certain she stiffened and looked stunned. Because she did. But that didn't stop Russell. He caught onto the back of her neck and hauled her to him.

He kissed her!

She didn't fight him, though she considered it, but decided to wait and see where this was going. However, she got her pepper spray ready just in case.

He moved his mouth over hers as if this were something they did every day. He was good at the facade. Very good. And for just a split second Julia's body reacted to the man who was doling out that one, hot kiss.

And, sadly, he was hot, too.

In that split second, she understood the attraction that had no doubt drawn Lissa to him. She hated it, especially since she was feeling it herself. But she understood it. Russell Gentry, with his butt-hugging jeans, cowboy boots and too-long hair, was the kind of man who reminded a woman that she was indeed a woman.

A reminder she never wanted to feel again.

She slapped her hand on his chest, pushed him away and glared at him. But Russell only chuckled.

"Julia's upset that I missed the birth of our little one." Russell stared at her when he spoke. His tone was all light, but the facade didn't make it to his eyes. He was giving her a warning to stay quiet. "But she understands how important my work is. She knows I need to make a living. That's why she'll head out while we talk business."

Milo made a grunting sound that could have meant anything, and he didn't say a word for several moments. Julia felt every one of those moments in her held breath and racing heart.

"I have a better idea," Milo finally responded, and there was sarcasm in both his tone and body language. "You spend the evening with your girlfriend and baby, and I'll call you about another meeting."

"This meeting is important," Russell snapped. He was staring at Milo now, so she couldn't see his face, but Julia didn't need to see his expression to know Russell wasn't pleased. Whatever this meeting was supposed to be about, it was obvious he didn't want it postponed.

But she did.

Julia wanted out of there so she could get some answers and then call the police. It was entirely possible that Emily's father would be arrested before the night was over.

"The meeting can wait," Milo insisted. He motioned toward the ski-masked guy, who then darted out of sight. Milo turned to leave, as well, but Russell caught onto his arm with this left hand. The gun was still ready in his right.

Russell shook his head. "It can't wait. I have people already onboard for this deal, and they aren't into waiting. They want this to go down in the next twenty-four hours, or else they'll pull out. All that money will be gone, including your sizeable cut."

Milo looked down at the grip Russell had on his arm, and he didn't say anything until Russell released it. "I'll be in touch." And with that calmly spoken exit line, Milo turned and strolled away.

Russell cursed, stared at her, and then cursed some more. "Lady, you have no idea what you've just done."

Though he was furious and she didn't know if he would act on that fury or not, Julia still hiked up her chin and met him eye-to-eye. "Oh, I have an idea. I stopped something illegal from happening."

The stare turned to a glare, and he grabbed her arm. "Come on. Did you leave your silver Jag in the bar parking lot?"

Julia blinked but didn't ask how he knew about her vehicle. He'd obviously noticed her earlier, when she was following him. Strange, he hadn't given any indication that he'd known.

"Why do you ask about my car?" she demanded.

"Because we're going to get in it, that's why, and then we can have a serious chat about how you just screwed up everything I've worked so damn hard to put together."

She didn't even have to think about that proposal. "No, we're not doing that. And I don't care a rat's you-know-what about screwing up any of your plans. I'm also not getting in a car with you, but we *are* going to get some things straight right here, right now."

But where should she start? There were so many questions. So many concerns and fears. Julia started with the most recent one.

"You told that man, Milo, who I was. Why? Why not just give him a fake name the way *you* did? Now he knows who I am, and I would have preferred someone like that to not have any personal info about me."

Russell continued to volley cautious glances at both ends of the alley, but he also huffed to let her know he wasn't pleased about her not budging. "Milo saw your driver's license in your purse."

Of course. It was right there. Russ had looked at it himself, just minutes earlier. That took a little of the fight out of her.

"Unnecessary lies cause unnecessary suspicion," he added. "Trust me, you don't want to make a man like Milo more suspicious."

He glanced at the sidewalk again and eased his gun into the waistband of his jeans. "And you don't want to hang around in this alley. I'll walk you to your car, and then I'll watch you drive out of town. We can have the rest of this conversation over the phone."

Russell Gentry expected her to leave. And what she wanted was nothing more than to get away from this man and whatever was happening—but not before she had the answers she'd come for.

"Did Lissa know you were a criminal when she slept with you?" she asked angrily.

This was supposed to be a quick trip to turn over custody of Emily, but Julia had no idea what to do now.

This might end up in a custody battle, though she seriously doubted that Russell had a burning desire to raise a newborn.

He used the grip he had on her to get her moving, much as he'd done in the bar. "I told you I don't remember your cousin, so I have no idea what she knew or didn't know about me. Other than Lissa's word on her deathbed, what proof do you have the baby is mine?"

"DNA proof," she snapped.

That stopped him, and even though they were now on the sidewalk where Milo and his henchman would see them if they returned, Russell stared at her. "Impossible."

She was too scared and angry to be smug. "No. The P.I. who followed you around San Saba took a coffee cup you used, and the lab compared it to Emily's. There's a ninety-nine-point-nine percent chance that you're Emily's biological father. And I stress the biological part, because anyone, including the likes of you, can father a child."

He blew out a slow breath, and even though he didn't dispute her claim, he didn't jump to announce that he was indeed the birth father. There wasn't just doubt in his eyes, there was total disbelief.

"Look, I don't know if you're trying to scam me, or what," he said, his voice low and somewhat threatening. "And at this point, I really don't care, other than to warn you that scamming me isn't a good idea."

"Why would I lie about something like this?" she asked, not waiting for an answer. "No one with any common sense would want you to be an innocent newborn's father. If I had any doubts whatsoever about that,

I don't have them now. I know what you are, and I don't want you anywhere near Emily or me."

He stayed in deep thought for several moments. His forehead bunched up. His mouth slightly tightened. "Is the baby here in San Saba?"

Baby Emily was with a temporary nanny in Julia's hotel room, but she had no intention of revealing that to Russell. It'd been a mistake to bring Emily. But Julia hadn't known she would be walking into a vipers' nest.

"She *is* here," he insisted. And he cursed, the words even more vicious than before. "The baby is here in San Saba." He kicked at a piece of broken beer bottle on the sidewalk, and he got her moving again in the direction of the bar—and the parking lot that was on the other side.

"It doesn't matter where Emily is, you're not going to see her," Julia informed him. "You're a criminal, and I'll fight you with every breath in my body to stop you from getting anywhere near her."

Of course, she hadn't actually counted on becoming a permanent guardian to the child, but at the moment Julia didn't think there was another option. Not for her, and definitely not for Emily. She could return to her San Antonio estate with Emily and lock them both away from Russell and his cohorts. With her money and connections, she could be sure to keep him away.

She hoped.

He didn't say a word. Not when they passed the bar. Not when he hauled her into the parking lot and toward her car, which she'd parked directly beneath the lone security light. While they walked across the cracked concrete of the parking lot, he used the remote button on her keys to open the car door. He maneuvered her inside behind the wheel and shoved the key into the ignition.

She considered just driving away as fast as she could, but Julia first wanted to get something crystal clear. "You won't challenge me for custody. Because no judge would give a baby to a criminal like you."

The muscles in his jaw stirred. He opened his mouth, but before he could answer, something caught his attention. It caught Julia's attention, too. It was a slow moving black car creeping past the parking lot. Because of the darkly tinted windows and the poor lighting on the street, Julia couldn't see the driver, but she got a bad feeling that Milo or the ski-masked guy had returned.

"They're watching you," Russell mumbled, more to himself than her. And then he repeated it in the same tone as his profanity.

"What does that mean?" Julia was afraid of the answer.

He scrubbed his hand over his face and groaned. "It means Milo is suspicious."

She didn't think it was her imagination that he was carefully choosing his words and having a mental debate about what to say next. An angry mental debate.

"What I'm about to tell you," he finally said, "you have to keep secret, and if you do tell anyone, you'll be arrested for obstruction of justice. Got that?"

No. She didn't get that. Julia shook her head. "What's going on?"

"I'm not a criminal." Another pause, and she could see the mental debate continue. "I'm Special Agent Russ Gentry, FBI."

Julia's mouth dropped open. "What—"

He reached inside and used the central latch on her door to unlock the passenger's side. Before she could stop him he got inside.

"You just walked into the middle of a dangerous undercover investigation," he snarled.

He pressed the control pad on her key chain, and the locks on the doors snapped shut. "You'll be lucky, damn lucky, if I can get you out of this alive."

Chapter Three

Russ watched the chain of emotions slide across her face. First total, undeniable skepticism. She didn't believe him. Then, her eyebrows drew together. She eased her gaping mouth shut.

And then reached for her phone.

Russ would have bet a month's paycheck that she would either do that or try to slap him again. The latter still might happen if she didn't get the answers she wanted to this paternity issue. Russ wanted those answers, too but right now, both their butts were on the line. God knows who Milo had alerted about this wrinkle in their plan.

"If you tell anyone who I am," he reminded her, "I'll arrest you."

She pushed his pointing finger aside. "And you can't expect me to blindly accept what you're saying without confirmation. I'm calling Sentron Securities. The owner will be discrete."

Maybe. Maybe not. Russ knew *of* the owner, Burke Dennison. And Sentron seemed to be an above board operation. But he sure as hell didn't want his cover blown.

He had to establish his identity so he could force

Julia to cooperate. He could probably force her anyway, but it would take time and cause a scene. Julia was an heiress, and he couldn't very well force her into protective custody without someone asking the wrong questions.

"Make your call to Burke Dennison," Russ conceded, but he shot her another warning glare. "But put it on speaker and be very careful about what you say."

She pressed some buttons on the cell, waited and stared hard at him.

"Burke, it's Julia Howell," she said, to the person who answered. She placed her purse on the console between them. "I need a favor, but this has to stay between us."

"Absolutely." The man's voice was clear over the speaker. "What is it?"

"Russell Gentry might be a government employee. Could you check?"

"Contact Silas Duran at the FBI," Russ said, in a loud-enough voice for Burke to hear. "He'll brief you, then debrief you, and if you give the information you learn about me to anyone but Julia Howell, expect a full-scale investigation that will land your butt and Sentron in scalding hot water. Got that, Dennison?"

There was a pause, or more likely a hesitation from Dennison. "Give me a minute." Finally, he said "I'll call you back."

"Start driving to your hotel," Russ told Julia. He reached over to turn the key in the ignition. Not the brightest idea, since she batted his hand away and in doing so, his arm grazed her breast.

That earned him a glare. And it would have been better if she'd let out an outraged gasp, rather than that breathy feminine sound similar to the one she'd made after he kissed her.

That kiss had been a stupid idea, too.

Even though Julia Howell was perhaps a liar and a boatload of trouble, she was attractive, and damn it, his body wouldn't let him forget that. She was making him hot. Well, she and the Texas heat. He could feel the sweat trickling down his back. Julia wasn't immune to it, either, because she blotted the perspiration from her face.

Since they appeared to be staying put for a while, Russ got started on more damage control. "Who knew that you picked up Lissa's baby from the San Antonio Maternity Hospital?"

She pulled back her shoulders. "Why?"

Man, she doesn't give an inch. "Don't make everything hard. Just answer the question. Who knew?"

Her shoulders went back even more, and she continued to glare at him. "SAPD, of course. And several members of the medical staff."

Russ groaned. "Reporters?"

"No. I paid a lot of money to keep the details of Lissa's story quiet. Her death was initially reported, and her name was listed in the newspapers, but I asked everyone to hold off mentioning the baby."

"And they cooperated?" he asked, stunned.

"Yes. I told them I didn't want you to learn you were a father by hearing it on the news. I wanted to tell you in person."

Well that was something, at least. Half the state didn't know the truth about the baby, and that meant Russ could slant the info in his favor.

Russ took out his own phone to make another call

to FBI headquarters in San Antonio. He asked to speak to a computer tech, and it didn't take long for Denny Lord to come on the line. "I need you to doctor some files for Julia Elise Howell."

"What?" she snarled.

Russ ignored her. "People will be digging into her background, and I need you to plant information that she recently gave birth to a baby girl. Keep all details vague, as if she tried to keep the pregnancy hush-hush. Doctor a photo if necessary. Oh, and let me know if anyone does any deep searches on her."

"What was that about?" she demanded, the moment he was off the phone.

"It was about making the story I told in the alley mesh with what Milo's people will learn about you." He only hoped it was enough. "By the way, it's not a good idea for us to be sitting in this parking lot."

"And I don't think it's a good idea to be driving to a hotel with you. I don't trust you," Julia snapped.

"I don't trust you, either, since I think you're trying to scam me. Or kill me from dehydration. Turn on the AC."

"If I do that, it'll only encourage you to stay. I don't want you to stay. I want you to get out." She blotted her upper lip again.

"Well, I'm staying until I get some clarification about why you chose me for this…well, whatever the hell it is."

However, Russ rethought that. Julia had money, so why would she come after him with this ridiculous daddy claim? "But right now the scam is on the back burner. First we deal with the fallout from the meeting in the alley."

"No. First we deal with your identity."

"I'm an FBI agent," Russ repeated, "and you're messing with an investigation that's taken me a long time to put together." And it could all be in the toilet, thanks to a prissy San Antonio heiress and her baby charades.

"Does your investigation have to do with black-market infants?" she asked.

He laughed, but not with humor. The woman had nerve…or something. "I'm not discussing one detail of my investigation with you. You've already overheard way too much."

"Or maybe I've overheard the dealings of two criminals meeting in an alley to discuss selling a baby." She swiveled around and faced him. "Do you have a badge?"

It took him a moment to answer, because when she swiveled, her dress slid up a little, and he got a visual reminder of her great thighs.

"Not with me. It's generally not a good idea to carry a badge while undercover. Bad guys tend to kill you if they find out you're an FBI agent. Imagine that." He didn't bother to tone down the sarcasm.

With a mighty effort, he forced his attention off her thighs.

She tipped her head to the ceiling and groaned softly. Finally she started the car. She turned on the AC, but didn't put the car into gear. "If you're lying to me, somehow I will make you pay."

Russ leaned into the AC vent and let the cold air spill over him. "Ditto, darlin'. Except, there is no *if* in what you're saying. It's a lie. I didn't sleep with your cousin and I'm not her baby's father."

Julia put her face closer to her vent, as well. "The DNA says otherwise."

Yeah? It did? Well, it did if she was telling the truth about that. Of course, that went back to motive. Why would she lie about something like that? He wasn't rich, and he had no prospects of getting rich anytime soon.

And then it hit him.

Russ snapped back from the AC vent. "You said something about using my photo for facial recognition software. Where is that picture?"

"In my purse." She tipped her head toward it.

He couldn't get to it fast enough. Russ rifled through the gold bag and came up with three photos. One was of the baby, which he'd already seen. The other was a young twenty-something brunette who resembled Julia. Cousin Lissa, no doubt. But it was the final picture that grabbed his attention and sucker-punched him.

Suddenly, all of this became crystal clear.

"Let me guess," Russ said. Though he wondered how he could speak with his jaw suddenly so tight. "Lissa called her baby's daddy 'RJ'?"

She shrugged. "Yes. So?"

Russ started to groan, curse and hit his fist against the console, but he knew none of those things would undo what had apparently happened nine months ago.

"RJ, as in Russell James," Julia interjected. "As in *you*."

"As in *Robert Jason* Gentry." Those words had been even harder to speak than the others, and despite all the anger and frustration, he couldn't help but feel the pain, too. It'd been months, and it was still there. Fresh and raw.

Russ figured it always would be.

"Who's Robert Jason?" Julia asked, suddenly looking as dumbfounded as Russ felt.

He reached in his pocket and took out his wallet so he could extract the only photo he carried. It wasn't standard procedure to carry personal photos while in a deep cover situation, but Russ hadn't had the heart to take it out. He did now, and passed it to Julia.

She studied it, but Russ already knew every little detail. It'd been taken nearly two years ago, on a rare fishing trip they'd managed to schedule.

It was the last time he'd seen RJ.

"You have a twin brother," Julia mumbled.

"Identical twin." Which explained the match in the DNA. Identical twins didn't have the same fingerprints, but the standard DNA test couldn't distinguish one from the other.

She shook her head. "But your brother didn't come up during Sentron's search."

"He wouldn't have. RJ is…*was* black ops for the CIA. It would have taken more than Sentron or a traffic camera to find anything on him. All of his real records were sealed years ago."

Her gaze slashed to his. *"Was?"*

"Was," Russ repeated. And he repeated it again to give himself time to clear the lump in his throat. "He was killed on assignment nine months ago, probably just days after he met your cousin. He's the reason I was in San Antonio at that bank. I was the beneficiary of his estate, and I had some paperwork to sign."

"He's dead," Julia mumbled. But she continued to volley glances between the photo and him. "And you really are who you said you are—Russell Gentry?"

"Russ," he said, automatically making the correction. Russell had been his dad's name, and he wasn't comfortable calling himself that.

The answer had no sooner left his mouth when her cell rang, and in the dimly lit car, he saw Sentron Securities flash on her caller ID screen.

Russ merely motioned for her to answer it.

"Burke," she said, placing the call on speaker. "You have something for me?"

"Julia, he's telling you the truth. Russell Gentry is an FBI agent."

She pulled in a hard breath. "Thank you, Burke."

"I'm sorry about this, Julia. We dug as deep as we could go, and we didn't find his FBI records."

Russ cut off what sounded like just the beginning of an apologetic explanation. "Silas Duran will clear up loose ends with you," Russ informed the security specialist, and he reached over, took her phone and clicked it off.

"I'm sorry—" Julia began.

But he cut her off, too. "Sorry won't help. The only thing that will help is damage control, and that's about to get started."

Julia nodded and handed him back the picture. "What can I do?"

"For now, you can go back to your hotel, take the baby and return to San Antonio. Did you fly or drive here?"

"I drove. Emily's only two weeks old. She's too young to fly."

Well, in some ways that made it easier. No trip to and from the airport, but that meant she had to go about a hundred and fifty miles to get home safely.

"You have some kind of security system, I assume?" he asked.

Another nod, but her eyes widened with alarm. "You think Emily could be in danger?"

She shoved the car in gear and darted out of the parking lot. The tires squealed and kicked up bits of rock that spattered against the car. She didn't stop there. She grabbed her cell and made another call.

"I need to speak to the nanny. Don't worry. I won't mention you," she explained. "Zoey," she said, when the nanny answered. "I need you to make sure the door is locked. Don't let anyone in until I get there."

Julia ended the call, but she continued to mumble to herself.

Russ actually welcomed this high level of concern. It might get her to cooperate. "The baby's probably not in danger...*probably*," he emphasized. "But I don't want to take any chances." He carefully placed the photo back in his wallet and put it in his pocket. "After all, she's my niece."

Russ mentally repeated that. He was an uncle.

Later, he'd come to terms with that and the fact that RJ had fathered a child he'd never seen, never even known about. But that had to wait.

"I have a security system," Julia explained. "Supposedly, it's the best money can buy. And I can hire bodyguards. I'll do whatever it takes to keep Emily safe."

Russ nodded. "I'll arrange to have an agent or a cop follow you home. And once I've wrapped up things down here, I'll contact you."

She had a white-knuckle grip on the steering wheel. "Milo can't hurt her."

She was taking his warning very seriously, but there was no reason for Milo to go after Emily.

Because she looked ready to lose it, Russ reached over and skimmed his hand down her arm. Why, he didn't know. After everything she'd just learned about him, his touch probably wasn't very comforting.

"How badly did I mess up your investigation?" Julia asked. She stopped when the light turned red and drummed her fingers impatiently until it turned green. She gunned the engine.

"I can salvage it," he assured her.

But Russ wasn't certain of that at all. Still, he had no choice but to try.

Julia pulled to a quick stop in the parking lot of the Wainwright Hotel. Even though it had three floors, it was a fairly small building and only had about two dozen rooms. He'd already guessed that that was where she'd be staying, since it was the nicest hotel in a town that was seriously lacking nice things. The outskirts of the town were okay—more family oriented; and more likely than not, if you were in downtown San Saba, you were looking for trouble.

"Let me call my partner, Silas Duran," he told her. "He can make the arrangements for a security escort, and I can wait with you until everything is in place, so you can leave."

"You trust this Silas?" she asked.

Russ nearly gave her an automatic yes—but stopped. He settled for a nod.

Silas was a fellow agent and probably well trained. But Russ didn't like that Silas had only been on this case for a couple of days. He also didn't like that Silas might have pulled strings to get the assignment. That's the way it seemed to Russ, anyway. But that was a problem for him to mull over when he had more time.

She opened her door and looked at him. She nibbled lightly on her bottom lip, caught it between her teeth for several seconds. "I suppose you want to see Emily?"

He did. But the timing was all wrong.

Or was it?

Russ didn't know how long it would take to get this investigation back on track, and he couldn't leave San Saba until Milo put him in touch with the head honcho—the slimeball only identified as Z. Russ wanted to find Z and lock him away for a long, long time for what he'd done. If it took him weeks or longer to do that, it would be weeks before he first got to see his niece.

"Yeah," Russ heard himself say. "I'd like to see her. I won't stay long."

He had to pay an uncle's tribute to his dead brother's child and give Julia a promise that he would be back as soon as he could.

Since Julia was obviously too anxious to stay put any longer, Russ took out his phone and called Silas while they made their way into the hotel. He also kept watch around them, and breathed a little easier, once they made it into the lobby.

"Russ," Silas answered, "I was just about to call you."

Oh, no. Even though he'd only been working with Silas a short time, he knew that tone, and this wasn't good news.

"Where are you now?" Silas asked.

"With Julia Howell." Ahead of him, Julia made it to the elevator and jabbed the up button. "She's about to leave for her estate, but I need to request a security detail for her."

"We have a problem. She can't leave," Silas said.

Russ hoped he'd misunderstood. "What do you mean?"

"I mean she can't leave. If she does, this investigation is over, and you get to start it from scratch."

Because he might lose signal in the elevator, Russ clamped onto Julia's arm to stop her from stepping into it.

"I need to check on Emily," she insisted.

Russ pulled her to the side so he could continue this conversation, a discussion that he was positive he wasn't going to like.

"Explain," Russ told Silas.

"Milo just called his contact to set up another meeting for tomorrow afternoon. We can choose the exact time and the location."

Russ relaxed a little. Maybe the investigation hadn't been ruined. Maybe he could rescue that baby after all. "Well, that's good. The meeting's critical." And it was critical they control the location so they could set up security.

"No, it's not good." Silas said, cursing. A first. He had never heard Silas use even mild profanity before.

Russ listened to Silas's news. Yep, it was bad all right. And a few moments later, he was doing his own cursing. "Can we change Milo's mind?" Russ asked.

"No. Believe me, I tried, but he was adamant. We can take extra precautions. We can even bring in a few more agents. So the question is, do you think you can talk Julia Howell into cooperating?"

Russ looked over her at and saw the nerves right

there at the surface. He could possibly convince her to do what Milo wanted. *Possibly.* But even if they controlled the security and the meeting place, it didn't mean something wouldn't go wrong. Julia could ultimately be in more danger than she already was.

If that was possible.

Milo would dig to find out who she was, and then he'd wonder why an heiress worth fifty million would get involved with a lowlife like Jimmy Marquez. By doctoring her records, they could make it work.

Well, maybe…if they could convince Milo that Julia had a thing for slumming or bad boys.

"The stakes are too high to fail," Silas reminded him.

Yeah. And that was the real bottom line.

One way or another, even if he had to resort to begging, even if he had to put her in more danger, Russ had to bring Julia deeper into this.

Because a baby's life depended on it.

Chapter Four

The moment Russ ended his call, Julia got them into the elevator. Everything inside her was starting to spin. Her breathing was too fast. Her thoughts were going a mile a minute.

She tried to make herself slow down, so she could think this through, but the only thing that kept going through her mind was the importance of keeping Emily safe. Later, she'd berate herself for coming here to San Saba before she had thoroughly assessed the dangers. Julia had been in such a hurry to carry out Lissa's dying wish that she hadn't considered that some dying wishes just couldn't be fulfilled.

This was obviously one of them.

She had to grab Emily and leave the minute Russ had a security escort in place.

When the elevator door finally opened, Julia rushed out. She fished her keycard from her purse and slid it into the lock as soon as she reached the door. Then she hesitated—looked back at Russ, who was right on her heels.

"What?" he asked. After a moment of studying her face, he cocked his eyebrow. "Trust me, I'm having second thoughts about being here with you, too. But unless you got a time machine in that purse, we can't go back to the bar and undo what happened."

True, but Julia still didn't open the door. "Just how much are things messed up?"

"They're messed up," he answered. Now it was his turn to hesitate. "But I swear I'll do everything humanly possible to keep Emily safe."

Julia nodded. That was something at least. "You should know, I don't handle danger well. Old wounds." She added "Literally." Out of breath, she knew she had to get control of herself.

He touched his fingers to his chest. "Does this mean you're about to have a panic attack or something?"

"No," she snapped.

That wasn't exactly the truth. She might have one. It wouldn't be the first.

"I'm not sure what it means. I just thought you should know that alley meetings and having guns pointed at me aren't things I can handle."

"You already have," he reminded her.

"Things I can't handle *again*," she said. "*Or* after the fact. I usually don't break during the heat of the moment, but afterward, all bets are off."

Russ stared at her, and that stare reminded her of how close they were. Not as close as in the alley of course, but still close enough. He was a disturbingly attractive man, and the sooner she got him out of her life the better.

He huffed, cursed under his breath and reached out to touch her arm, as he had earlier. A sort of gentle rub, with just the tips of his fingers. It had worked then. A small miracle. But she was too close to the edge for it to work now. Still, she didn't move away from him.

"When I was seventeen I was attacked." Her words rushed out with her breath, and she felt her heart pounding. Her chest began to hurt. And she had no idea why she was telling him any of this. "A date went wrong. My parents had warned me that the guy was bad news. I didn't listen. I thought I knew more than they did. And when the guy tried to rape me, and he couldn't, uh, perform, he stabbed me three times and left me to die in the trunk of my car."

The tears came, and she cursed, used the profanity to quell the building anger. She wasn't that naïve girl anymore. It wasn't worth crying or panicking over now. She'd been rescued twelve years ago, and was still alive.

"Shhh," Russ said, his voice so calm. He put his arm around her and eased her closer. Not quite a hug, but almost. "Want to show me your scars, and I'll show you mine?"

She went stiff and eased back a little so she could make eye contact. But he was busy lifting his chest-hugging black T-shirt. She got a good look at his toned and tanned chest, his tight abs and the scar just to the left of his heart.

"I know a little bit about being left for dead...and staying alive." He lowered his T-shirt. "So do you. That's good, Julia. Because I need you to be a survivor."

She smeared the tears off her face and narrowed her eyes. "What do you mean?"

He opened his mouth as if he were about to answer, but then he shook his head. "Let me meet my niece first, and then we'll talk."

She just continued to stare at him so, he reached around her and opened the door. Or rather, he tried to do that. The nanny had obviously put on the safety latch and chain.

"It's me," Julia called to Zoey.

"Julia, thank God you're here. You scared me with that phone call." Zoey opened the door, but she stopped when she spotted Russ. Probably because Russ looked… well, dangerous.

And was.

"Everything's okay," Julia said, trying to assure the woman. "I might have overreacted." She hoped she had, anyway. Julia motioned toward Russ and shut the door. "This is Russ Gentry, Emily's *uncle*."

Zoey's dark brown eyes widened, and she looked him over from head to toe. "What happened to the birth father?"

"My brother was killed," Russ replied, as he double-locked the door.

"Oh." The young woman probably didn't realize that her mouth had dropped open. She stayed that way for several moments. "Well, I'm sorry. And I'm sorry for Emily. She's barely two weeks old and already an orphan."

Yes. She was. The poor thing. Julia would soon have to figure out what to do about that orphan status. She'd need to contact her attorney and see what the process was to become Emily's permanent legal guardian.

Julia thought of her old baggage. The old wounds. They were the reason she'd given up the idea of having children of her own. She hadn't wanted to bring a child into her world of panic attacks, nightmares and fear. A "recluse," the press called her. Well, while that might be good enough for her, she couldn't raise a child in a vacuum.

The idea caused her to take a deep breath.

"Emily's still asleep," Zoey explained, stepping to the side. "She hasn't woken up since you gave her the bottle before you went out to talk with Mr. Gentry."

That wasn't a surprise. Emily slept a lot, and when she wasn't sleeping she was eating, fussing and requiring a diaper change. Still, with all that work involved, Julia hadn't expected to find the baby to be so enthralling. She had tried not to let herself get attached, but there was nothing to hold her back now.

"This way," Julia told Russ, and she led him through the small living area, in the direction of one of the bedrooms in their three-room suite. Julia had had the crib moved into her own room so she could stay up nights with Emily. Zoey was using the other.

The door was already open, and the lamp was on, so she had no trouble gazing fondly at Emily in the crib. Julia automatically smiled—and she was glad for that reason to smile. With the incident in the alley, she needed something to bring her back to normal, and Emily had a unique way of doing that.

With Russ right next to her, she tiptoed closer and stared down at the baby. She was so precious, with her light brown curls and pink cheeks.

"Her eyes are brown," Julia whispered to him. Like Russ's eyes, and no doubt, his twin brother's. Now that they were side-by-side, Julia could see the resemblance even more. Emily definitely had the Gentry DNA.

"Despite the circumstances of her birth, she's very healthy." Julia gave the pink blanket an adjustment that it didn't really need. She just needed to touch the baby. "She weighed seven pounds, three ounces when she was born, but she's already gained nearly a pound."

When Russ didn't say anything, she looked at him. But he didn't seem to notice that she was even in the room. His attention was focused on Emily.

"She's beautiful," he whispered. He touched Emily's hand lightly, and she closed her fingers over his thumb. He sucked in his breath. "She's like a tiny angel."

There was so much emotion in his voice, Julia had to do a double take to make sure Russ Gentry had spoken those words.

He had.

This was the man who had stared down gunmen in the alley?

He was turning into a marshmallow right before her eyes.

"Oh, man," he mumbled. The smile started in the corner of his mouth and spread until it was a full grin. "I didn't expect this."

Julia didn't need clarification. She'd had the same reaction when she first saw the child.

"The love," he said. "It's instant. I mean, it's like my blood knows that she's my niece."

She understood that, too, but she suddenly became very uncomfortable.

She thought Russ would do a quick peek and head back to the sitting room so they could have that talk he'd mentioned. But this was no quick peek.

He drew back his hand so he could scrub it over his face. He groaned softly. "Okay. I can deal with this. I can make it work."

"Make what work?" Julia asked.

He tipped his head to Emily. "I was due to move to a supervisor's job in the next year anyway, but this will just speed things up. I'll get out of undercover work when I'm done with this case."

"What do you mean?" Julia said that a little louder than expected.

He shrugged, as if the answer was obvious. "A desk job in the San Antonio office will give me regular work hours. And it'll be safer. I can have a more normal life. And I can finally get a haircut," he added, shoving the strands of hair away from his face.

Julia put all those things together. *Oh, no! He couldn't mean* that. "Are you saying you want to raise Emily?"

He gave another shrug. "Of course. She's RJ's daughter. My niece. I'm her next of kin. Who else would be raising her?"

"Me," Julia blurted out.

That erased any trace of Russ's goofy smile. "You're her cousin. I'm her uncle, and her father was my identical twin brother. That's a closer bloodline than you have with her. Besides, if Lissa had wanted you to raise her, she would have said so."

It felt as if someone were squeezing a fist around Julia's heart.

"Lissa said that because she thought Emily's father was alive. And because she probably thought I didn't want children. She was wrong. Besides, need I remind you that you're in the middle of a dangerous investigation?"

"An investigation that'll end soon." He stared at her. "You want to raise her yourself?"

Julia managed an indignant nod. "Well, I am the natural choice."

That was far from the truth, but Julia wasn't speaking with her head. This was a *heart* thing.

"Why? Because you're a woman? Because you're rich?" he asked, challenging her. "I can feed her a bottle and buy her clothes just as well as you can."

Since this was obviously about to turn into a nasty argument, Julia gave Emily's blanket another adjustment and caught onto Russ's arm so she could lead him out of the room.

Zoey was there, apparently waiting for an update, but it would have to wait. "Could you excuse us?" Julia asked her, then waited until Zoey was in her room before she continued.

"What makes you think you'd be a good father?" Julia demanded.

"Maybe the same thing that makes you think you'd be a good mother," he countered. "I love Emily. It doesn't matter that I just saw her for the first time, I love her."

"And I don't suppose it matters that the dangerous elements of your job could follow you from undercover work to a desk?"

"The FBI makes it a priority to protect the families of their agents."

She was about to launch into the next wave of the argument, but he lifted his hand in a stop-right-there gesture. "Look, this isn't a good time to go at each other about custody. We can work that out later."

"Can we?" she snapped.

"We can," he calmly assured her. Russ glanced around the room, and his attention landed on the minibar. Next to it was the small microwave she'd had brought in so she could heat up Emily's formula.

"Do you have any hard liquor?" Russ asked.

Julia was still in a fit of temper, and that trivial-sounding question didn't help. "Help yourself."

"It's not for me. It's for you." He went to the bar, selected a bottle of bourbon and poured some into a glass. He brought it back to her and motioned for her to sit on the sofa.

Because Julia's legs were still wobbly, she did. She also took the drink and had a sip, despite the fact that she hated bourbon. As expected, it watered her eyes.

Russ eased down on the sofa next to her. Not on the other side. But practically hip-to-hip with her. So close that she could see the trouble brewing in his eyes.

"This drink is to help pave the way for what you need to tell me," she said.

He nodded and combed his gaze over her. "I'm physically attracted to you. That'll be a problem—"

"What?" The remark was such a surprise that it took her a moment to continue. "This is what you needed to tell me?"

"No. It's just FYI. I keep thinking about your lace panties. I keep thinking about kissing you. That'll be a problem because I'm a guy, and in my mind, that attraction will get all screwed up, and I'll have this overwhelming need to protect you. I can't have that now, because there's someone else I have to think about."

Julia had another sip of the bourbon and was disgusted that she needed it. "Am I supposed to understand that?"

"Yeah. Because I'm pretty sure you're attracted to me, too."

She tried to deny it. Tried hard. But the lie wouldn't make it past her throat. "I won't get involved with you."

No lie there. It was the truth. Julia didn't get involved with anyone—ever.

"Good." He didn't seem insulted. More like *relieved*. "Because I need to ask you to do something, and I don't want sex, lace panties or attraction to have any part in your answer."

She stared at him. "You're not making sense."

"I will, soon." He took the drink from her and finished it. "Milo, the gunman from the alley, contacted my partner to set up another meeting."

"Good." She nodded. "You said the meeting was important."

"It's more than important. And Milo won't go through with it unless I bring you with me."

Julia felt her heart skip a very big beat. "W-what?"

"Normally, I wouldn't have even considered it, but the stakes are astronomical. Besides, if I don't bring you, Milo will be even more suspicious. He might panic and do something stupid. Something that could set things back worse than they already are."

Oh, God. Julia wished she'd finished that drink after all. Her heart started racing. She could feel the adrenaline flash through her. The anxiety hit her like a ton of bricks. She was racing toward a full-blown panic attack.

"Just take a deep breath," Russ said, as if knew exactly what she was experiencing. He caught onto her chin. "Don't make me put my hand up your dress again."

"What?" She pushed him away from her.

"That's right. Get mad. Slap me if it'll help. Hell, kiss me. Do whatever you need to do to stop that response. It's old garbage, and you're stronger than you think, Julia. I watched you in that alley, and if I thought for one minute that you couldn't handle this, I wouldn't be asking."

She blinked. No one had ever accused her of being strong. And much to her surprise, it worked. She felt her heart rate ease back to normal.

"That's good," Russ mumbled. "And for the record, I've never threatened to put my hand up a woman's dress before. Well, not unless it involved mutual foreplay."

A nervous laugh escaped before she could stop it. But she had nothing to laugh about. *Nothing.* Russ had just told her he wanted her to meet with a dangerous criminal.

"What's at stake at this meeting?" she asked.

He met her eye to eye before he answered. "A baby's life."

Russ said it so softly that it took a moment to sink in. Julia gasped. "A baby?"

He nodded. "A child just a little older than Emily." Russ took a deep breath. "I'm at the tail end of an investigation. Milo thinks I'm a black-market baby buyer, and that my client is someone rich, but who doesn't have the credentials or the background for a legal adoption. Milo's boss is the seller, a man whose identity I need to know so I can stop him from doing this again. Or it's entirely possible that Milo is working alone. Either way, he has the baby."

"Then why not just arrest Milo and make him tell you where the baby is?"

"Because he'll just deny it. And if he's put in jail, he'll have his hired guns take the baby, go in to deep hiding, and we'll never see the child again."

She touched her fingers to her lips to stop them from trembling. "Where did they get the baby?"

"They stole him from his parents, Aaron and Tracy Richardson. And they left a note, warning the parents not to go to the authorities or the baby would be harmed. Thankfully, the Richardsons called the cops and the FBI anyway, because we learned that Milo or his boss intended to sell the child all along—probably by pitting the buyer he thinks he has waiting against what the parents will shell out. The baby will go to whoever pays the most."

Julia hadn't thought this day could get any worse, but she'd obviously been wrong. "My God."

"Yes, I've been saying that a lot lately myself. People are messed up, Julia, and they do disgusting things. If I don't complete this sale and get the baby, then Milo will find another buyer, and the little boy will end up being sold. Maybe he'll get lucky and get good parents. Maybe he won't. We know from past deals that Milo has been very careful about the buyers he chooses."

Julia didn't feel a panic attack, but her heart broke at the thought of an innocent child being bought and sold. "And if I don't go…"

"The meeting won't happen." He lifted his shoulder. "Not unless I can somehow reason with Milo."

She'd already seen him fail to do that in the alley, when Milo had cancelled the meeting. A cancellation that'd happened because she was there. If she hadn't chosen this night to approach Russ about Emily, then the stolen baby might have been rescued and on the way back to his parents.

"How safe will this meeting be?" she asked.

Russ took a deep breath. "We can set up security in

the area to take out any of Milo's men if they make a wrong move. I don't think they will. This is about the money. Milo wants the huge middleman fee, and I think he'll play nice to get his hands on the cash."

Julia stayed quiet a moment and gave that some thought. "And what would I have to do?"

"Maybe just stand there and look beautiful. Which won't be a stretch," he added, in a mumble.

She hated that she felt flattered with that ill-timed compliment. "Then why does Milo want me there if I'm just to be your arm dressing?"

Now it was Russ's turn to have a few moments of silent thought. "Could be several possibilities. He might already know you're a rich heiress. He might think you're the actual buyer instead of Silas Duran, the agent we have in place for that. Or he might just want you there because he believes it'll be safer for him."

"Safer how?"

"If Milo suspects this is a sting operation, then he could see you as a shield of sorts. The FBI wouldn't go in with guns blazing if you're in the line of fire."

"This is a lot to put on you," Russ continued. "I'll understand if you say no."

If she said no, Julia couldn't live with herself, but if she said yes, she might not make it through the meeting without a panic attack. Still, she would be there. She would fulfill Milo's demand, and if she had an attack, so what? It would be humiliating for her, but it might speed things along with Milo. Besides, there really wasn't a choice here. Julia knew what had to happen.

"I'll do it," she heard herself say. "Just tell me where I have to go and what I have to do."

Russ didn't seem surprised that she agreed. He

simply nodded and gave her another of those arm rubs.

"We'll know the details of the meeting in the morning," Russ explained. "For tonight, there'll be an agent outside your room. I won't leave until he arrives."

"Where's the stolen baby right now?"

Russ shrugged. "We don't know. But I'm sure he's fine. The deal is to deliver a healthy baby boy to the buyer."

That was something at least.

Julia heard the soft sound. It was barely audible, but it got her to her feet so she could go to the bedroom. Emily was stirring in her crib.

Russ got up, too, and followed her. "She's awake."

When Julia reached the crib, she saw those big brown eyes staring up at her. The baby looked first at Julia, then at Russ.

"Hi, princess," Russ said, before Julia could say anything.

But he didn't stop with just a greeting. Russ reached down into the crib and picked her up. He didn't hesitate, and he didn't say something clichéd about being afraid she'd break. He eased Emily right into his arms, cradling her protectively against him, and he rocked her as if he'd done this a thousand times.

"What?" he said, defensively, when he glanced at Julia, who was staring at him.

She had several questions she was trying to ask at once. "Do you have children of your own?"

"No. And I'm not married, either. Never have been. But I love kids. Always have."

Obviously. "This isn't your first time holding a baby, is it?"

"Hardly. Most of my coworkers and friends have kids. I'm godfather to three of them. All boys." He leaned down and gently kissed Emily's forehead. "What about you? Do you have much experience with kids?"

"Plenty," she lied. Truth was, Emily was the first and only baby she'd ever held.

He chuckled when Emily puckered her lips. "I rescued a little boy not much older than her just three months ago, and I held him for hours before we could get him back to his parents. He was a cute kid all right, but nothing like the little angel here."

Rescued? So, the stolen baby wasn't his first. She supposed that made Russ a hero of sorts. And he certainly seemed to be a natural with Emily.

My God. She could actually lose custody of Emily to him. Yes, she had more money than Russ. Well, maybe. But she had also been in therapy for twelve years. She had panic attacks. And the final blow—Lissa hadn't asked her to raise Emily. She'd wanted Julia to merely be the locator, and Lissa had murmured that dying wish in front of several members of the medical staff and a cop.

None of that would be in Julia's favor.

Still, she had to fight; and her first step was to put some distance between Russ and her. Between Russ and Emily. Out of sight, out of mind might help him realize that he didn't want to give up his undercover life after all.

"You're breathing fast again," Russ pointed out. But he didn't look at Julia when he spoke. He kept his attention on Emily and made cooing sounds.

Cooing!

"I was thinking about Lissa," Julia mumbled, and forced herself to breathe normally.

"You were close to her?" He didn't wait for an answer, as he announced "The angel just smiled."

Julia looked at the baby, who did indeed seem to have the right corner of her mouth lifted into a pseudo-smile. Her first. And she'd smiled for Russ, not for her.

"Lissa and I weren't close," Julia admitted. "But we used to be."

"Before the attack," Russ added when she didn't say more.

A cooing hero with ESP. Great. This wouldn't be a custody battle, it would be a custody war.

"Yes," she finally answered. "It was Lissa who set me up with the guy who stabbed me. He was a friend of hers." A friend from the wrong side of town, her parents had said. Lissa had been from the wrong part, too. That's what had drawn Julia to her. And look how that had turned out.

Russ pulled his attention from Emily and looked at her. "You blame Lissa for what happened to you?"

"No. But she blamed herself. We weren't close after that, and I was too broken to try to mend things between us." Uncomfortable with yet another personal wound that she hadn't intended to reveal, she reached out and took Emily. "It's probably time for a diaper change."

Now, that should send Russ running, Julia thought. But it didn't. "I can do it," he said, when Julia placed the baby in the crib. "With my godsons, diapering can be a challenge. I've gotten hosed down more than once."

He reached into the bag next to the crib and pulled

out the wipes and a diaper, but he had barely gotten started when his phone rang. The sound shot through the room and startled Emily. Julia picked her up again before she could break into a full-fledged cry.

Russ glanced at the caller ID on his phone. "I have to take this." And he stepped back into the sitting room.

While Julia finished up the diaper changing, she tried to hear Russ's conversation. But she couldn't tell anything from his monosyllabic answers. It was possibly about the security guard who would be assigned duty outside her door. Or maybe it was about the meeting with Milo.

The meeting she hoped she wouldn't regret.

Of course, she would have regretted not trying to save the stolen baby even more.

"I understand," Russ said. He ended the call and came back into the room.

"Is the security guard here?" she asked.

"He is." Russ reached down and ran his fingers over Emily's toes. "But there's a problem."

Her head whipped up, and she met his gaze. "Not the baby?"

"No. Not the baby. My partner, Silas, just informed me that Milo has one of his men staked out near the hotel."

Her heart dropped. "You don't think his man will try to get in here?"

"No reason for him to do that. He's watching us with an infrared thermal device."

"A what?"

"It means he can see us. Not complete images, but the heat that our bodies are generating." Russ turned and slipped his arm around her waist. He eased her closer. "It means Milo is trying to figure out if you really are my fiancée."

Sweet heaven. Her first instinct was to jump back from Russ, because it made her skin crawl to think that someone was spying on them. But Russ held on to her.

"What do we do?" she asked.

"I stay here tonight." He tipped his head to the bed. "There. With you."

Chapter Five

Russ stared at the laptop and tried not to break the screen.

Silas had sent him the reports and pictures on Julia's computer, since Russ didn't have his own with him. And the FBI hadn't wanted to risk having one delivered to the hotel, in case it would make Milo even more suspicious. If that was possible.

Russ wasn't feeling good about Milo's meeting. But then, he was feeling even worse about the pictures in front of him.

They were photos of Julia's attack.

Everything had been documented by the San Antonio police and used to convict the SOB who'd done this to her. There it all was—the details of the assault with a deadly weapon, the position of each stab wound, every bruise and scrape.

She'd been damn lucky to survive, because any one of the stab wounds could have hit a vital organ. Added to that, she'd nearly bled to death in the trunk of her car. A passerby, out walking his dog, had heard her moaning and rescued her. It'd been cold that night, close to freezing, and the low temperatures had slowed her bleeding.

Julia was alive because of a freak cold spell and a dog who needed a midnight walk.

In other words, blind luck.

Russ wasn't able to hold back his feelings any longer, and he mumbled some profanity. Her attacker had gotten a life sentence, but that didn't seem nearly harsh enough for what he'd done.

Beside him, Julia stirred a bit, pulling the cover to her chin, but she went back to sleep. Good thing, too. They'd been up and down most of the night, with Emily feeding every four hours. Julia had taken the midnight shift, and after he watched how she prepared the formula, he did bottle duty at 4:00 a.m. Since it was going on seven, it wouldn't be long before Emily woke up for the morning round. She might be a little angel, but she ate like a lumberjack.

He smiled at that thought. It'd be like having daily miracles, just watching her grow up.

Russ closed down the files on Julia's stabbing, and then deleted them from her computer. He didn't want her coming across them accidentally, even though she probably remembered every single detail in those reports. He certainly remembered the bullet that had landed him in a hospital bed for over a week; but as an undercover agent, bullets were a possible job hazard. Julia had been attacked on a date. Big difference.

Julia stirred again, moving from her side to her back, and shifting the comforter in the process. That shift exposed her breasts. She was wearing a gown and a robe, but the robe had opened, and he could see the outline of her nipples.

Too bad Milo's infrared couldn't read Russ's dirty thoughts. There would have been no doubts about Julia being his fiancée. Well, Milo wouldn't have had doubts about the attraction being real, anyway.

Oh, it was real, all right.

And the bed sharing hadn't helped. It also hadn't helped that he'd slept on top of the covers so there wouldn't be any skin-to-skin contact between them. All through the night, Russ's body hadn't let him forget that he was in bed with an attractive woman.

Thankfully, Russ didn't have to pretend to have sex with her. Since Milo thought Julia had given birth just two weeks ago, that gave Russ and her an excuse not to take the pretense to the next level.

Russ saw her eyes open. There was that sleepy flash of ice blue, before she gasped and tried to scramble away from him. She obviously wasn't accustomed to waking up in bed next to a man.

He didn't say anything, just gave her a few moments to pull out of the sleepy haze.

"Oh," she murmured, and she swiveled around so she could see Emily.

"She's still asleep," Russ whispered.

Julia made a small sound of relief and sat up, her robe shifting again. He caught a glimpse of the scar at the top of her right breast.

She looked at his damp hair and his bare chest. "You showered already?"

He nodded. "About an hour ago. I washed out my shirt, since I don't have a change of clothes." He'd been as quiet as possible, so he wouldn't wake anyone. And then he'd gotten some work done on her laptop. "I figured, with only one bathroom, I'd better get in and out before Zoey or you needed it."

He glanced at her breast again and bit back a groan.

"Any news about the meeting?" she asked. Was it his imagination, or did she dodge looking at his chest, as well?

"No. Silas should call soon." He paused and tried not to look at her. "Are you having second thoughts?"

"Yes," she admitted, "but I'm going through with it anyway."

"You're a brave woman," Russ said.

"Right. Remind me of that when it looks as if I want to turn and run."

Oh, he would. But what he couldn't seem to do was keep his mind off her breasts.

Julia's gaze dropped down to her partially exposed breast, and she gasped again. She tried to cover it up, but Russ caught onto her hand.

"It's okay," he said, keeping his voice emotionless.

She shook her head and her eyes watered. She obviously wasn't used to anyone seeing her old wounds.

Russ didn't think. He just leaned over and dropped a kiss on the scar. The moment his lips touched her warm, musk-scented skin, he knew it was a whopper of a mistake. His sympathetic brain was trying to assure Julia that she was beautiful, with or without scars, but that stupid, brainless part of him below the waist assumed this was foreplay.

He got rock hard.

And he waited for Julia to slap some sense back into him.

But she didn't.

She caught onto his face with both hands. Maybe to stop him from kissing her again, but she didn't push him away, and she kept her touch gentle. She stared at him with those now-hot-blue eyes.

"I can't," Julia whispered. "I mean, I haven't. I won't...and I can't."

Russ tried to process that semibabble—was she saying she was a virgin? It would fit. The attack had left her with physical and emotional scars. But the virginity didn't fit with the rest of her. She was beautiful by anyone's standards, and certainly, after twelve years, some guy had to have been able to help her get past the wounds and make love to her.

"Never," she added.

Or maybe not.

"Oh, man. You've obviously crossed paths with your share of...jerks." Though that was mild, compared to what he wanted to call them. "Never?"

"Never," she snapped. "It's no big deal. I've never wanted to have sex. Not since the attack, anyway."

Maybe she didn't want to, but she had admitted she was attracted to him.

She pushed him away and tightened the robe back around her. That was his cue to drop the subject—and to ice down the hot blood he had for her. She certainly didn't need a man with his track record. He was thirty-three and hadn't dated a woman for more than two months at a time.

"Change the subject," she insisted.

"Okay."

Russ moved the laptop to the nightstand and looked at her—at the white terry-cloth robe she was gripping like a full-body chastity belt. And he knew he should just back off and leave this alone. But then he thought of Milo's man watching them. Except, that was more of an excuse than anything, because mainly, he just thought about kissing that not-wanting-to-have-sex lie right off Julia's mouth.

He leaned in and their breath met. Julia got that deer-caught-in-the-headlights look, but she didn't move away. So he got even closer, until his mouth hovered over hers.

And he waited her out.

"All right," she snarled. She slapped her hand on his chest and pushed him away. But not nearly far enough. Besides, with her hand on his bare skin, it only made things more intense. "Maybe I do want you. But because I want something, it doesn't mean it'll happen. You're not my type."

"You're not mine, either."

Though it seemed true for both of them, he was still hard—and she seemed to be going softer, hotter and breathier with each passing moment. Everything kicked up another notch when her fingers moved. Just a little. But enough to glide through his chest hair. Maybe she wasn't even aware of the touching, but he certainly was.

His phone rang, the sound shattering the insane moment. Russ fumbled to get his phone from his pocket so he could answer it before it woke Emily. But he wasn't successful, because Emily immediately started to cry.

Julia sprang from the bed to get the baby, and Russ answered the call, because he knew it would be from Silas and therefore important. He only hoped he didn't sound as out of breath or aroused as he actually was.

Damn, he'd let Julia get under his skin.

"How's baby-and-heiress duty?" Silas greeted,

probably because he heard Emily fussing. But Russ didn't care for the man's tone.

"It's all right. Better than I thought it'd be." And much to Russ's surprise, that was the truth. He hadn't minded the short sleep time in between feedings.

Julia was another story. If he had to sleep next to her again, it would require multiple cold showers and maybe a big rock that he could use to hit himself in the head.

"Well, I hope you're rested," Silas continued, "because its shaping up to be a full day. The meeting with Milo is all set at the state park at two p.m. I won't be on the park grounds, because I want to stay out of sight, but I'll be nearby, in case you can close the deal."

So it was on schedule as planned. If Milo agreed to the one-million-dollar offer for the baby sale, then Silas was to arrive on the scene as the buyer. The next step was to get Milo to agree to a time and a place for the exchange. Silas would get the baby, and Russ would follow Milo or his henchmen back to his boss, Z. If there was no Z, and Milo was the sole person responsible for taking the baby, then Milo would be arrested.

With luck, they could have the baby by nightfall. And Julia and Emily would be safely on their way back to her estate. After that, Russ could, well, he could get his own head on straight so he could figure out how to approach the whole custody issue.

"So, is Julia Howell onboard for the meeting?" Silas asked.

"She is," he said, though he was beginning to have more doubts about it all. "Please don't tell me Milo's made any other crazy requests."

"No. Not so far. But there has been a hitch. I'm in the lobby of the hotel where you're staying."

"Why?" Russ demanded. "You know Milo has a man watching us."

"I do. And he's still there, parked less than a block up the street. I came in through the back. Neither Milo not his man would recognize me, and I didn't know if you wanted to keep it that way."

"I do." Since Silas was going to pose as the buyer for the infant, Russ didn't want Milo asking questions about why Silas had been at the Wainwright, where Julia was staying. "So why did you come?"

"I had no choice. Twenty minutes ago I got a call about someone else who was already here at the hotel."

"Not Milo?"

"No. The stolen baby's parents, Aaron and Tracy Richardson. I have them waiting in the manager's office, but I don't know how long I can talk them into staying put. The mother is nearly hysterical."

Russ almost dropped the phone. "The parents? How the hell did they end up in the Wainwright Hotel in San Saba?" Russ tried to keep his voice down, but it was hard.

"My fault. They've been calling me for updates every hour, and yesterday I let it slip that we were in San Saba."

"You what?" Russ couldn't help it. He cursed.

"I didn't mean to tell them," Silas insisted, his voice suddenly louder. "It just happened. The mother was crying. The father was yelling. I was just trying to assure them that we were close to finding their baby."

"And you did that by giving away our location," Russ

growled. "Did you also let it slip that *I* was here at the hotel?"

"No. But when they told me they were coming to San Saba, I said I'd meet them. I just went there to calm them down. Russ, they were scared, and I didn't want them going to every hotel in town looking for me. That would have sent plenty of red flags up for Milo's men."

Yeah, it would have, but the parents' arrival at the Wainwright would be a massive red flag on its own.

Russ had to get his teeth unclenched so he could speak. "Please tell me you didn't meet the parents here, when you were trying to calm them down?" One meeting was bad enough, two would be a disaster.

"No. I met them at a café on the other side of town. I was careful, but the parents had someone follow me. And he must have been good, because I didn't make him. He followed me straight to the Wainwright Hotel."

Russ shook his head. "When were you here at the Wainwright?"

"Last night."

Well, that was news to Russ. "Why?"

"I was going to do the security detail to escort Julia Howell, but by the time I arrived, I got the call about Milo and the meeting."

And Silas hadn't told him this, even though it could be a huge problem. "You risked Milo and his men seeing you here twice," Russ pointed out.

"That's why I went in the back. I was careful. But if Milo brings it up, we can just say that since I'm the buyer, I've been meeting with you to discuss the money and the details."

That sounded logical, unless Milo was already suspicious of Silas. "This changes the plans for the meeting. Even if the deal closes today, I don't want you to come waltzing in there while Julia's around. We'll wait until she leaves."

"If Milo agrees to that," Silas said.

Yes. Milo might be a problem, but they were going to have an even bigger problem on their hands if their covers were blown.

"I hope you told the parents they put their baby in more danger by coming here," Russ asked.

"I told them, but they aren't listening. They aren't leaving either. They're demanding to talk to *you* now."

"Why me?"

"Because they believe you're the one who'll be in direct contact with the seller."

That was true. Russ would be in direct contact with Milo. But that didn't mean he should give in to their demands and meet with them.

"My advice?" Silas added. "Listen to what they have to say, because they're claiming they have new information about who has their son."

Chapter Six

Julia changed Emily and started the bottle, but her attention was on the phone call that Russ had gotten. She could tell he was talking to Silas, but the conversation wasn't going well. Something had obviously gone wrong.

Zoey came out of her room, glanced at Russ and then joined Julia. "Is there a problem?" Zoey asked.

"Too many to name," Julia mumbled.

And after the all the danger, one of the biggest problems was Russ. She'd thought their relationship was already complicated enough, but that breast kiss had sent this crazy camaraderie spinning out of control. She needed to attend the meeting with Milo so she could take Emily and get far away from Russ. She couldn't think when he was around.

Russ finally ended the call and walked into the sitting room, but he didn't offer an immediate explanation as to why his forehead was bunched up with worry. Zoey obviously noticed there was a problem, because she took Emily and the bottle into her bedroom.

"Well?" Julia asked Russ, when he still didn't say anything.

"The stolen baby's parents are here at the hotel."

Surprised, she shook her head. "Was that planned?"

"Not even close." And his tone and body language indicated it wasn't just unplanned, it might be a huge complication. He went into the bathroom, and when he came back out, he was putting on his shirt. "I need to talk with them, because they might possibly have some new information about the case, but I want to make it look like a social meeting."

Julia thought about that a moment. "You want me to go with you?"

"I don't want you to go," he said, gritting his teeth, "but I think it's better than any alternative I can come up with. I certainly don't want to meet with them here, with Emily in the next room. And since Milo's man is still watching, I don't want him to get the idea that I'm doing a deal with another seller. That might send him to look for another buyer."

Julia nearly laughed. Not from humor, but from the irony of the situation. Two weeks ago, she'd been closeted away at her estate, only leaving a couple of times a year when it was an absolute necessity. She had even arranged to have her therapy sessions done at the estate.

Now, here she was in the middle of a dangerous FBI investigation. And while she was scared for Emily and herself, she was more frightened of not being able to get the stolen child back to his parents.

"What do you need me to do?" she asked. She sounded far more certain of herself than she was, but Russ likely knew that.

"First, get dressed. I'll give you instructions on the ride down in the elevator."

Julia forced herself to move. She hurried into the

bedroom, grabbed a wine-colored, loose-fitting dress, and sandals from the closet. She wasn't sure what a person was supposed to wear to a clandestine meeting, but she dressed as quickly as she could, put on some makeup and brushed her hair. When she finished, she found Russ talking to Zoey. Specifically, telling her to double lock the door and not let anyone in.

That nearly caused Julia to panic.

"You think Milo's man will try to sneak in here?" she asked and then held her breath.

"No," Russ answered, quickly. "But just in case, there'll be an agent in the hall outside the room. He's posing as a housekeeper."

Good. Julia would help with this investigation, but not at the expense of Emily's safety.

Russ took her by the arm and led her out of the suite, but he didn't leave the door until they heard Zoey engage both locks as Russ had instructed.

"After the two o'clock meeting with Milo, my plan is to get you and Emily out of San Saba," he explained, on the way to the elevator. He nodded to a man wearing a hotel uniform, who was in the room next to the suite changing sheets.

The undercover agent, no doubt.

"You think Milo will agree to me leaving?" she asked.

"He'll have to. One meeting is bad enough. I don't want you involved with this any longer than necessary."

"I don't want to be involved, either, but does that mean you think you'll have the little boy by this afternoon?"

"It's possible, but even if it's not, you and I are going

to stage an argument for Milo." He turned and faced her while they were in the elevator. "I want you to call me all the names you've been thinking about calling me. I want you to say it's not going to work between us, and for me to get out of your life. And then I want you to leave. An agent will keep an eye on you when you go to your car, and someone will make sure you get safely back to the hotel."

That didn't seem difficult, but it left a lot of things unanswered, too. "Then what?"

"The next part will be easy. You'll take Emily and Zoey, and leave for the estate. I'll get the Richardson baby and hand him over to his parents."

That was exactly what she wanted to hear. So, it might all be over by early afternoon. Julia didn't want to think beyond that, but she was certain this wasn't the last she'd see of Russ Gentry.

Once this investigation was over, he would return to San Antonio and challenge her for custody. The anger came with that reminder, and she could already think of some names to call him in front of Milo, when Russ and she had their fake argument.

"As for this meeting with the Richardsons, I'll just introduce you as my fiancée," Russ continued. The elevator doors swung open, but he caught onto her arm to stop her from stepping out. "And don't say too much around my partner, Silas. He's the one who told the Richardsons where we were."

Julia couldn't believe what she'd just heard. "What?"

"Yeah. That was my reaction, too. He's either incompetent or…" But Russ didn't finish the thought. "Don't worry. I've arranged for extra security for you at the meeting. I don't intend to rely on Silas for anything."

Great.

So, she was walking into a meeting with terrified parents and an idiot agent who was possibly dangerous. Julia checked her hands. She wasn't shaking, and she didn't feel a wave of panic. Maybe she'd had so much anxiety dumped on her in the past twenty-four hours that her body was adjusting.

"By the way, you look hot," Russ mumbled to her, a split-second before they walked into the café off the lobby.

"So do you," she mumbled back, and was pleased that it actually caused him to pause a step. She was betting not too many things off-balanced a man like Russ.

Russ smiled at her and ushered her toward the trio seated at a table in the corner. A tall blond woman immediately jumped from her chair.

"Her name is Tracy Richardson," Russ told Julia, in a whisper. "She's the mom, and I want you to greet her as if she were an old friend."

Julia did. She walked to the woman and pulled her into a hug, probably surprising everyone at the table, especially Tracy Richardson.

"We need to look friendly and cozy," Russ whispered to all of them. The other two men stood, as well. "Because we almost certainly have an audience."

Julia glanced around the small café and didn't see anyone suspicious, but that didn't mean Milo's man wasn't using the infrared device to watch them.

"Aaron." Russ greeted the father in a louder voice. They shook hands. "Julia's told me all about you." The thin-faced man was dressed to perfection in a dark blue suit, white shirt and Ivy League tie. He had old money written all over him, and being from old money herself, Julia recognized it.

Since the man in the suit was Aaron Richardson, that meant the other man was Silas Durant. Like Russ, she wouldn't have picked him out of the crowd as an agent, which was probably why he was one.

Silas was around six feet tall and heavily muscled, as if he'd once played football. He was younger that Russ, probably by at least five years, and he wore khakis and a pale blue shirt. Unlike Russ, who still wore jeans and a black T-shirt. His rough haircut and attire was probably the reason he'd wanted her to pretend to be friends with the Richardsons.

"I ordered all of us coffee," Tracy said, her voice shaking.

Everyone sat, but Russ's gaze was firing everywhere. He was keeping watch.

"You said you had information about who might have taken your son?" Russ prompted. He kept his voice low, and held the coffee mug in front of his mouth.

"We think our nanny, Marita Gomez, might have been involved," Tracy said.

Russ exchanged glances with Silas. "But we checked on Ms. Gomez and cleared her as a suspect. Yes, she was with your son when he was taken, but she was also clubbed on the head and had defensive wounds. It seems to us that Marita Gomez did everything within her power to stop your son from being taken."

Aaron shook his head. "Tracy found a note."

Tracy reached into her purse and produced the folded piece of paper. "It's not an actual note. I went through Marita's room and saw this pad of paper on the desk, and I thumbed through it. I didn't see any writing, but I saw these indentations on one of the last pages of paper, so I used a pencil to rub across it."

Russ unfolded the paper, and Julia glanced over and saw the numbers.

"It's a phone number," Aaron explained. "But it's probably for one of those prepaid cells that can't be traced."

"How do you know that?" Russ asked.

"Because I tried to call it, and when no one answered, I phoned directory assistance. They said the account didn't have any minutes remaining, so it was no longer active. Now, why would Marita have been calling someone with a prepaid phone?"

Julia could think of one reason—maybe the nanny was phoning a friend who just happened to have that type of cell service.

"If you thought this was important," Russ said, "you should have turned it in to the FBI office near your home in Houston."

"We couldn't. I had to see you, to show you." Tracy's voice was still a whisper, but the low tone couldn't conceal the emotion.

"Tracy." Julia reached across the table and placed her hand on the woman's. "It'll be okay. They'll find your son."

Tracy stiffened, probably because she didn't care for the intimate gesture offered to her by a stranger, but she finally nodded. "Silas said it could all be over soon. I pray he's right."

From the corner of her eye, Julia saw Russ scowl. Like her, he was probably wondering what else Silas had told them that he shouldn't have.

"Here's what I need you to do." Russ set down his

coffee cup and directed his comments to the Richardsons. "I need you to go home and wait."

"You're not helping by being here," Silas added. "In fact, you could jeopardize the plan for us to rescue your son."

Tracy gasped, and tears instantly sprang to her eyes. Beside her, her husband didn't make a move to comfort, her as Julia had done.

"We can put up more money," Aaron told Russ. "When you meet with the buyer, offer him two million."

"Three," Tracy insisted. "Or more. Offer him whatever he wants. I just want Matthew back safely with me."

Aaron didn't immediately jump to agree to that, but he finally nodded. "Offer them whatever's necessary."

"Money might not be an issue if the seller loses trust in me," Russ pointed out. "So, finish your coffee, hug Julia goodbye, and then leave. If anyone asks, you were in town on business and dropped by the hotel to say a quick hello to an old friend. That's it."

Aaron gulped down the coffee and shook his head. "I knew we shouldn't have come. I told Tracy, but she wouldn't listen."

"Because you didn't listen to me," Tracy fired back. "I can't sit around like a block of ice, waiting." She looked at Julia. "I just can't."

Julia could relate, unfortunately. If Emily had been taken, she would have done worse than shown up in the San Saba. She would have P.I.s out searching for the baby, and no one—not even the FBI—could have stopped her.

Tracy took a sip of coffee and seemed to calm down a bit. "I'm sorry. I haven't been myself since Matthew was taken. I shouldn't have had the nanny take him to his pediatric checkup. If I'd been with him, I would have fought to the death to stop them from taking him." Her pale green eyes landed on Russ, then Silas. "You're doing your best. I know that. But please check on the nanny. Make sure she wasn't calling the person who stole Matthew."

"Let's go," Aaron insisted, getting to his feet.

Tracy stood, too, and as Russ had instructed, she gave Julia a hug. "Please," she whispered to Julia. "Bring my baby back to me."

"I'll try," Julia promised. She watched them walk out of the café, and then sank back in her chair next to Russ. "What now?"

But Russ didn't answer. His attention was on Silas. "We'll talk later," Russ said. And it sounded like a warning.

"You have a right to be upset—" Silas started.

"I said we'll talk later," Russ interrupted.

Silas looked ready to argue, but his phone rang. He glanced down at the screen and then excused himself so he could walk to the other side of the room and take the call.

"You don't trust him?" Julia asked, following Russ's suddenly stony gaze that was aimed at his partner.

"I'm not sure." He blew out a weary breath and scrubbed his hand over his face. "But then, I'm not sure I trust the Richardsons. Meeting them was a real eye-opener."

"What do you mean?" she asked.

"I mean they put their son in more danger by coming here. They're not stupid, and they should have known that."

"True, but I think they're working from a purely emotional level. Well, Tracy is anyway. I'm not so sure about Aaron. He seems immune to her tears."

"Yeah. Their marriage doesn't seem to be on solid ground, does it?"

Julia agreed. "This might seem like a callous question, but why are you, as the intended buyer, offering so much money for the child? I mean, won't the large amount make Milo suspicious? Because I suspect someone greedy and resourceful, like your theoretical buyer, could go into a poor neighborhood and buy a child for far less than a million."

Russ nodded. "That happens. But Milo's selling the Richardsons' baby as a blue blood. Solid genes. Good potential. And the other thing Milo's got going for him is that, initially, he had more than one buyer. Or so he said. We think it was a ploy to pump up the price, but he turned down our initial bid. When we upped the price, it was accepted."

"Accepted," Julia mumbled, in disgust. And if Russ had been a real baby broker, then the money would have been exchanged, and the child would be forever lost to his parents.

Julia wasn't in the mood for coffee, but she drank some, and hoped the caffeine would ease the headache she had from lack of sleep. "Will you do more checking on the nanny?"

"I will. And I'll check more on the Richardsons, too...." The last part of that trailed off, because Silas returned to the table.

The man didn't sit, and there were beads of sweat on his upper lip. "We have a problem."

Russ groaned. "Not with Milo."

"Yes, Milo," Silas confirmed. "That was one of his henchmen on the phone. Milo wants to change the time of the meeting."

Julia's stomach clenched. "Not another delay?"

Silas shook his head. "Just the opposite. Milo says the meeting happens now, or it doesn't happen at all. He's giving you fifteen minutes to get to the state park. If you're not there, then the sale is off, and he finds another buyer."

Chapter Seven

Russ pulled Julia's Jaguar into the space at the far end of the parking lot of Mendoza State Park. In the hurried instructions he'd gotten on the drive over, it was where the head of the security detail, Chris Soto, had told him to park. It was a spot where the agents could keep Julia and him under surveillance.

But it was also a spot that left them out in the open.

Russ wasn't sure he liked that. Yes, it would make it easier for security to keep an eye on them, but he felt too exposed. Normally, he would have just accepted it as part of the job, but with Julia there, he didn't want to blindly accept anything.

"The fifteen minutes are nearly up," Julia pointed out. For the entire ride, she had her attention fastened to her watch.

Time was indeed running out, but Russ still took a moment to check their surroundings. He didn't see any agents on the security detail, which was probably a good thing, because that meant they were adequately hidden. But there were people milling about—families using the playground equipment and joggers on the red gravel track that wound through the park.

If Milo was indeed planning some kind of attack here, he'd have to do it in a very public place. Hopefully, Milo wouldn't want to draw that type of attention to himself.

"Here's the one rule you have to remember," Russ told Julia, "if anything—and I mean anything—goes wrong, you run for cover."

She nodded and drew in several shallow breaths. She was pale and trembling, too, but she didn't look to be on the verge of a panic attack. Well not yet, anyway. The meeting hadn't even started.

He checked to make sure his gun was in place in the slide holster at the back of his jeans. It was. Milo might search him and find the weapon, but Milo already believed that Russ was no saint. The man would no doubt expect Russ to be armed. Of course, Milo might also demand that Russ surrender the gun, but that was something he'd deal with if it came up.

Russ opened the car door, and Julia got out with him. Russ waited until she was by his side before they started the short walk to the picnic table that was just off a grassy path. Above the table was a flat, wooden roof, but the sides were wide-open.

Milo was there, sitting at the table and smoking a cigarette. And he wasn't alone. There was a tall, auburn-haired woman with him. Not seated. She appeared to be pacing. She wore a pale blue business suit. Which meant she could be carrying a concealed weapon.

"Who is she?" Julia asked in a whisper.

"I'm not sure."

Russ stopped, even though Milo and the woman had obviously spotted them, and he fired off a text message to Silas asking him for details. He hated to use Silas for this or anything else, but with the rush on the meeting, there hadn't been time to request another agent.

Sylvia Hartman, Silas texted back, *Milo's asst. Not armed.*

Good on the "not armed" part. But it did make Russ wonder why Silas hadn't called him about this possible glitch. Of course, with all the chaos going on to get Julia and him to the location, and arranging for an agent to guard Emily, Silas had likely had his hands full. For this, Russ would give the agent the benefit of the doubt.

"Jimmy," Milo greeted him. He didn't stand, nor did he put out his cigarette. But he did turn his attention to Julia. "So glad you could make it."

"You didn't give me a choice," Julia fired back.

Milo gave a brief, oily smile. "True. I thought your fiancé might want to speed things along if you were with him."

"And what about her?" Russ asked, indicating Sylvia. "Is she here to speed things along, too?"

"Absolutely," the woman insisted. "I'm Sylvia Hartman. I work for Milo."

She took what seemed to be a PDA from her purse, but it wasn't a PDA. Russ knew what was about to happen next.

Sylvia moved closer to them, and without actually touching them, she ran the device first over Russ. Then, Julia.

"They aren't wearing wires," Sylvia said to Milo.

"Are you?" Russ demanded of Milo.

"No need for one," Milo said calmly. "I can relay anything said here to my boss."

To Z, the real buyer behind all of this. And that

meant someone from the FBI would follow Milo from this meeting. So far though, following hadn't helped. Agents had tailed him the night before when he'd left the alley next to the bar, but the man had simply gone home.

"Now that I'm sure we can talk in private," Sylvia continued, "I can tell you that I've been dealing with the details of the *possible* transfer."

"Possible?" Russ demanded, aiming that at Milo and not his assistant.

"Possible," Milo repeated. "Why don't you sit, and we'll discuss it."

"I'd prefer to stand. And I'd prefer to hurry. Julia's anxious to get back."

"I'm sure she is." Milo let that hang in the air for several moments. "What, with her being a new mom and all. Hmmm. You certainly look good for a woman who just had a baby two weeks ago."

Julia shrugged and looked surprisingly calm. "I'll pass that along to my personal trainer."

Russ nearly smiled. Nearly. But he didn't care for the way Milo was studying Julia.

"If we're done with small talk," Russ started, "can we finally get down to business?"

It was Sylvia who answered, not Milo. "Sure. We assume your buyer is still onboard with this?"

Russ nodded. "Absolutely."

"Good. Because the exchange will take place tomorrow night, right here in the park."

Russ was shaking his head before she finished. "Tomorrow night? Why not sooner? The buyer's anxious to get this over with."

"Well, we're anxious, too," Sylvia insisted, "but it

can't happen before tomorrow. Logistics issues. I'm sure you understand."

"No. I don't, and my buyer won't be pleased." Russ didn't know how far he could push this. He wanted the deal to go down sooner than later, but he didn't want to blow it completely by not budging on the final hour.

"Well?" Milo questioned. "Does that mean everything is off?"

Russ took his time answering. Even though Milo seemed beyond calm, he hoped the man was as unsettled about this as Russ was. "Everything's on. What time?"

"Eight p.m.," Sylvia said. "Now, as for payment. The seller has had a change of heart."

Beside him, Russ felt Julia tense. "What the hell does that mean?" Russ asked.

"He no longer wants one million. He wants two."

Russ cursed. "For one kid? Come on. Two million?" Even though the Richardsons had agreed to that and more, Russ didn't want to put more of their money on the table if it wasn't necessary. "The agreement was for one."

Sylvia glanced at Milo, and he was the one to continue. "The seller is aware that the baby's parents might be willing to compensate him more than your buyer."

And this was something Milo would have known right from the start. "So why not just go to the parents?"

Milo gave another of those smiles and put his cigarette out on the table. "Because it's too risky. The parents have probably contacted the authorities, and any exchange might be…scrutinized. We'd rather deal with you and your buyer. The question is, would you rather deal with us?"

Again, Russ hesitated, and he looked at Julia to see how she was handling all of this. She was nibbling on her bottom lip, but there were still no signs of panic.

"I'll contact the buyer," Russ finally said. "But if he agrees to the substantial jump in price, then that's it. That's the bottom line. I don't want you jerking us around."

Milo stood and stared at Russ from the other side of the picnic table. "Ditto."

"Am I supposed to know what that means?" Russ made sure he looked Milo straight in the eyes when he asked that.

But Milo only shrugged. "Tomorrow. Eight p.m." He reached in his pocket and extracted a folded piece of notepaper. "That's the bank where we want the money deposited. Once we've verified the deposit, you'll get the goods."

"Not so fast," Russ tossed back. "Who will be at this meeting?"

"Me, of course. You. And Sylvia. The baby will be nearby."

"*How* nearby?" Russ demanded.

"Within minutes. Don't worry. We have no desire to keep this child any longer than absolutely necessary, and I'm sure your buyers feel the same."

"Buyer," Russ corrected.

But maybe Milo hadn't made a mistake. After all, the Richardsons had come to the hotel, and Milo could have figured out who they were. Milo might even believe the parents hadn't gone to the cops and were now in the running to outbid any other buyer to get their baby back.

"Right," Milo murmured. He walked closer and extended his hand for Russ to shake. Russ did, though he wanted to grab the SOB and beat the information out of him. Maybe before this was over, he'd get the chance to make Milo pay for this.

"Julia," Milo said, in the same tone as a goodbye. But he still took a moment to look her over from head to toe. It wasn't a casual look, but one from a man who was admiring the view.

Russ shot the man a glare. Yet another reason to beat him senseless.

Milo only smiled, turned and walked away. But Sylvia didn't. She stayed put and stared at both of them.

"Nothing can go wrong tomorrow night," Sylvia said, her voice practically a whisper now. And she certainly wasn't as calm as she'd been with Milo around.

Russ decided to push that lack of calmness a bit. "I don't want anything to go wrong, either, but my buyer is only willing to go so far. No more price jumps. No changes on the meeting time and place. This goes down just as we agreed."

She didn't nod, but she did swallow hard and walk closer. "There's a lot at stake here. Milo's anxious." Sylvia looked at Julia. "Mainly because of you. He didn't like that you just showed up here in San Saba when things were all coming to a conclusion."

"I didn't know about this deal," Julia insisted. "I came to tell Jimmy about the baby, that's all. I had no idea about Jimmy's deal with Milo."

"And I don't want her involved in this," Russ added.

"I especially don't want her at the exchange tomorrow night."

"I don't think it'll be possible to exclude Julia," Sylvia said, under her breath. She glanced around, as if to make sure no one was listening. Then, she moved even closer to Julia. "Milo is going to insist you be there."

Ah, hell. Russ was afraid this was going to happen. That's why he'd insisted on knowing who would be at the meeting. "Give me Milo's number. I need to talk to him."

"It won't do any good. As I said, he's anxious. He thinks this could all be a sting operation."

And Russ could perhaps thank the Richardsons for that. Milo might not have known who they were, but anyone's arrival at this point could have given him reason to be alarmed.

"For your sake, I hope it's not a sting," Sylvia continued. "Or anything else, other than a simple sale." She didn't direct that comment to Russ but to Julia.

"Is that some kind of warning?" Julia demanded.

"You bet it is." Sylvia gathered her things from the table. "Because Milo said, if anything goes wrong at the meeting tomorrow night, then he'll retaliate by taking your daughter."

JULIA TRIED NOT TO PANIC, but it was nearly impossible to stay calm. She didn't even wait for Sylvia to leave before starting for her car. She had to get back to the hotel so she could protect Emily.

While they ran, Russ took out his phone and punched in some numbers. "Lock down the Wainwright Hotel," he told the agent who answered. "Milo might try to take the baby from Julia's suite."

"It'll be okay," Russ told Julia, the moment he hung up. "Sylvia said Milo would only go after Emily *if* there was a problem with tomorrow night's meeting. We just have to make sure there won't be any problems."

Well, there was a huge one. Milo wanted her to be there, and Julia wasn't sure she could go through with it now. She wanted desperately to help the Richardsons get their son back, but she couldn't do that at Emily's expense. She had to take Emily and go into hiding, at least until Russ had all of this resolved.

She didn't want to think about how long that might take.

"An agent is outside your room," Russ reminded her when they reached the parking lot. But Julia could hear the concern in his whispered voice, and it was written all over his face.

She wanted to kick herself. Here she'd gone miles out of her comfort zone to keep the deathbed promise to Lissa, and now Emily might have to pay the price. This is what she got for taking a dangerous chance that she shouldn't have taken.

Russ used her keychain to unlock the car doors, and Julia hurried to get inside so they could drive back to the hotel. She wasn't far from the door, only about a yard away, when she heard the sound.

A loud pop.

At first Julia thought it was the sound of a car backfiring, but she thought differently when Russ yelled, "Get down!"

But he didn't just yell. He dove at her and pulled her to the ground. She hit hard, and her elbows and knees scraped against the rough concrete when Russ pushed her against the metal rim of her front tire.

There was another loud sound, and she saw concrete spraying from the pavement. And that's when Julia knew that someone was shooting at them.

She choked back a scream and tried to get up so she could get into the car, but Russ held her in place by crawling over her. He also drew his gun. He was obviously trying to protect her, but she couldn't see how that would help, especially if he got shot.

Or killed.

They could both die here. And *then* what would happen to Emily? Was Milo going after her right now? Was that what this was really all about? Maybe he wanted Russ and her pinned down like this so he could kidnap Emily.

Julia struggled, trying to get to the car, but Russ pushed her right back down until she was pressed against the tire. She couldn't figure out why he wouldn't let her just reach up and grab the door handle so she could jump inside, but she soon figured it out.

The next bullet landed just behind them and to the right, and it kicked up another spray of concrete and dust. Judging from the direction the bullet had come, the shooter was somewhere on the other side of her car.

Maybe *directly* on the other side.

There were other vehicles around hers, but it was hard to see. Worse, there were massive trees that towered over the park and the parking lot. The shooter could be in one of those or even in the two-story office building near the park entrance.

She heard someone yell, and all around were the

sounds of people running and calling for help. Hope-fully, no one had been shot, but if the gunman kept firing, there was a possibility of that. Julia remembered all the families and children she'd seen. Every one of them was at risk.

But the shooter only seemed to have Russ and her in his sights.

There was another shot. Then another. Both came too close and stirred up more concrete dust. It was hard to see. And even harder for Russ to return fire. With everyone now running and screaming, he couldn't risk shooting someone who just happened to get in the way.

But they couldn't stay put, either.

"Emily," she reminded him. She glanced over her shoulder at him, but his attention was darting all around the parking lot, including behind them.

"I know." He took out his cell and made another call. "Where is this SOB?" he yelled into the phone.

She was close to both Russ and the phone, but Julia didn't hear the answer because another round of gunfire drowned it out. The shot tore through the windows of her Jag, and pellets of safety glass fell to the ground beside them.

The next bullet came through the hood of the car.

It gashed through the metal and just missed Russ's head. Julia didn't want to know how close it'd come to killing him.

Russ ducked down, thank God, and yelled for backup to respond.

Julia prayed it wouldn't take long for that to happen. After all, backup should have already been in place. Well, if Silas had done his job, it should have been. She suddenly didn't like relying on a man Russ didn't seem to trust.

There was the squeal of tires, and from the corner of her eye, she saw a black car come to a jarring stop at the edge of the parking lot. Her heart dropped.

Was this Milo's men?

But Russ didn't move, and he didn't take aim at the two men who barreled out of the car. Both men were dressed in street clothes and were armed, one with a rifle and the other, a handgun. They took cover behind their vehicle but aimed their weapons in the direction of one of the massive trees. Russ aimed his gun there as well.

The shots stopped.

"The gunman's getting away," Russ spat out, adding a profanity.

He motioned toward the men who had gotten out of the black car, and one of them started to make his way toward Russ and Julia. Not in a straight line. He used some of the other vehicles as cover, and he inched his way across the parking lot until he got to them.

"Guard Julia," Russ told the man. "Get her back to the hotel."

Obviously, this guy was an agent, but she didn't understand Russ's "guard Julia" instructions.

Not until Russ moved away from her.

"I'll join you at the hotel as soon as I can," Russ said to her.

"You're not going after that gunman." She tried to catch onto his arm, but Russ shook off her grip.

"That's exactly what I'm doing."

Chapter Eight

Russ heard Julia beg him not to go, but he tuned her out so he could focus on the gunman. There was no way he was going to let this SOB get away with trying to kill them—even if that meant he'd have to do yet more damage control so he didn't blow his cover with Milo.

If there was anything left of his cover not to blow.

Someone had sent this gunman after Julia and him, and Milo was at the top of Russ's suspect list.

Somehow, he had to end this latest threat and gather all the pieces, so he could put them in place. But for now, his first priority was to stop a would-be killer.

He checked over his shoulder and made sure Julia was getting in the car with one of the agents. She was, but she wasn't going voluntarily. The agent was shoving her into the backseat of the vehicle. The adrenaline had ahold of her now. She was in fight mode, but it wouldn't take her long to remember that she needed to be back at the hotel with Emily. Once that happened, Russ could be sure both of them were as safe as they could possibly be.

It was up to him to make sure they stayed safe.

Ducking behind shrubs and playground equipment,

he looked in the direction of a clump of tall live oak trees. If the gunman was still there, the thick branches and leaves were hiding him; but Russ suspected he was already on the ground, or making his way down that tree as fast as he could.

He kept his gun aimed and ready, and he shouted for the park visitors to evacuate. He certainly didn't need a stray bullet hitting an innocent bystander.

Russ got beneath a tall metal slide so he could take a better look into those trees. But he saw no one.

His phone rang, and while he looked all around him to avoid an ambush, he also glanced at the caller-ID screen. It was Silas. Russ had a five-second debate with himself about answering it, but he knew he had to hear what his partner had to say. Besides, this call might be about Julia or Emily.

"Get out of there now," Silas told him, the moment he came on the line. "Milo had a man watching. He's waiting to see what you'll do."

"What I'm going to do is kill the SOB who fired those shots at Julia."

"You can't. I'm going in pursuit. Yeah, it'll blow my cover as the buyer, but Milo thinks the Richardsons are the real buyers anyway."

No doubt. But that was only one of the issues they'd have to resolve. "What about the agents who took Julia?" Russ asked. "Milo's man saw that happen, too."

"We'll convince him that they were your hired guns." Silas sounded out of breath, as if he had been running, but Russ couldn't see the man anywhere in the park. "We can create fake IDs for them and plant some bogus employment records that'll link them to you. They're waiting at the park entrance for you to get in the car."

His stomach dropped. "Waiting? I told them to get Julia to the hotel."

"I told them to wait for you. It's the only thing that makes sense, Russ. Now, get the hell out of here, or we might end up losing the Richardson kid."

Russ wanted badly to argue. Like Julia, he was primed for a fight, and he didn't want to let this shooter walk. Still, he couldn't blow the investigation.

He couldn't just turn and make a run for the car. Russ had to get out of the park in the same cautious way he'd come in—because it was possible the gunman was still in that tree waiting for an opportunity to shoot him.

Russ hurried. He didn't want Julia waiting out in the open any longer than necessary, and he finally spotted the black sedan parked on the side of the road at the entrance. Other vehicles were speeding away, and the San Saba cops were responding with seemingly every unit they had. The air was filled with the sound of sirens and people shouting.

The back door opened when Russ was just a few feet away, and he got in before he cops could see him. He didn't want to have to explain his gun or his lack of a badge. Especially since Silas had already warned him that one of Milo's men was watching.

Julia was the one who opened the door for him, Russ soon learned. She was there on the backseat, and she grabbed his arm to pull him inside so he could shut the door. The moment he did that, the agent behind the wheel drove away. Not speeding. He didn't want to do anything to draw attention to them so they'd be stopped. Russ's supervisor and Silas would be the ones to fill in the local police on what was happening.

"You're okay," she said, her voice filled with breath and nerves.

Was he? Maybe physically he was, but inside he felt as if he were battling a hurricane. He looked at the scrapes on her knees and cursed. "You're hurt."

She shook her head. "Just worried. I called Zoey. Emily and she are okay. For now."

That was good. But Julia was indeed hurt. He'd have to tend to those scrapes and check for anything more serious.

Unlike at the meeting, she looked on the verge of losing it. Russ hooked his arm around her and pulled her to him. "It'll be okay," he promised. But it was a promise he wasn't sure he could keep. Still, he would try, no matter the cost.

"We need to get to the Wainwright Hotel," Russ reminded the agents.

He knew both of them—Kevin Lopez and Chris Soto—and knew he could trust them. If they'd been available at the beginning of his investigation, he would have requested either of them for a partner.

"Silas," Russ mumbled.

"What about him?" Julia asked.

"He went after the shooter." Perhaps without FBI backup, since the two security detail agents were with Russ. But maybe Silas would get lucky and be able to apprehend the guy and haul him in for questioning. Russ had a dozen things he wanted to ask, including first and foremost—who had ordered him to fire those shots?

Unless Milo was the shooter.

That thought caused him to rethink his hired gun theory. Milo had left in plenty of time to get up in that tree. If he had a rifle already planted there, he could have been the one to take the shots. And if it was him, Russ would make him pay. As soon as the Richardson baby was safe, that is.

"Emily has to be all right," Julia whispered.

"She will be. But I have to move her to a safe house. You know that, right?"

There were tears in her eyes when she pulled back a little and met his gaze. "I know."

"Just hang on," he told her, and tightened his grip. All he could do was sit there and hold her.

Russ wanted to punch himself for allowing this to happen to her. Julia didn't need this in her head, not with all the other nightmares she already had to manage. Unfortunately, this new nightmare wasn't close to being over.

"Get started on the arrangements for the safe house and try to find some place local, so the move can happen ASAP," Russ told the agents, when they pulled to a stop in front of the hotel. "I also want any surveillance disks from the park. I saw some security cameras, so let's hope they were on and working."

"Anything else?" Chris Soto asked.

"Yeah. I need to speak with Milo. Find a way for that to happen. I don't have a number, because he uses only prepaid cells, but you might be able to reach him through his assistant, Sylvia Hartman."

The agents assured him they would get right on his requests, and Russ didn't waste any more time. He got Julia out of the car and into the hotel. The lobby had several people milling around, all of whom suddenly looked suspicious. Hell, everything was suspect right now and would be until he had answers.

There was a guard outside Julia's suite door, but Russ didn't dismiss him. He ordered him to stay put while he knocked and told Zoey to open the door. The woman did, and like Julia, she looked worried. Julia rushed past her and into the bedroom suite. Russ was right behind her, and they both saw Emily sleeping in her crib.

"You haven't had any visitors or calls, have you?" Russ whispered to Zoey.

"Just the call from Julia. Are we in danger?"

Because he didn't want to wake the baby, he took Zoey out into the sitting room. "No," he lied. "But as a precaution, I'm moving all of you to an FBI safe house. Don't call anyone. Don't tell anyone what's going on. I just need you to pack your things and get ready. Then wait in your room with the door locked and the curtains closed," he added.

Zoey gave a shaky nod and hurried toward her room. Russ then turned his full attention to Julia, who was no doubt ready for a panic attack. But he did a double take. Yes, there were the remnants of tears in her eyes, but she didn't have the pale, clammy look as she'd had after the alley meeting with Milo.

"I can't go to the safe house," Julia insisted.

"Excuse me?" Because Russ was sure he'd understood her.

She lifted her hands, which were scratched, and then quickly hid them behind her back when she noticed the damage. "If I'm not there for the meeting, Milo said it wouldn't take place."

He just stared at her. "After what just happened, I

don't intend to trust Milo about anything, much less a meeting that involves you being just inches away from him."

"Then what about the baby?" she asked.

Yeah. That was the two-million-dollar question. "If the shooter isn't Milo, then my next step is to call him. To tell him I don't trust him. I want his boss, Z, to find someone else to use as a go-between. Sylvia, maybe." Even though he didn't trust Milo's assistant, either. Sylvia might have given them the warning about Emily, but the woman was dirty by association, because no one legal and above-board would voluntarily work for a man like Milo.

"All I'm saying is I need to be available," Julia explained. Her voice broke on the last word. "And I can't be available if I'm shut away in a safe house. What if Milo wants another meeting in fifteen minutes? What if I'm not there and he finds another buyer?"

Russ was about to argue, even if the argument he had in mind made no sense, but Julia reached out and put her hand around the back of his neck. She pulled him down to her and kissed him.

In the back of his mind, Russ considered that she was kissing him to get him to shut up. He considered it. Accepted it.

And because he needed to feel her in his arms, he kissed her right back. The mouth-to-mouth contact didn't soothe him exactly, but it helped when he felt Julia's muscles relax a little.

The taste of her went right through him, turning his anger and rage into something warm. Something that felt too damn right for something so wrong.

He pulled back not because he wanted the kiss to

stop, but because he knew it shouldn't continue. He needed to check her for injuries, and it didn't take him long to find them. In addition to the scratches on her knees, there were some on her elbows, as well.

Russ double-locked the front room door and took her by the arm. "Come with me."

He had her sit on the bed, and he went to the bathroom to get a wet washcloth. The curtains were also closed tight, so he shut the bedroom door, too, and locked it. Double precaution since Emily was in the room with them. If he could figure out a triple one, he'd take it, too.

Russ knelt in front of her and got to work, trying to be as gentle as he could. Still, Julia winced.

"Sorry," he mumbled.

"It's all right. It has to be done." She kept her voice soft and low, probably so she wouldn't wake Emily. "I didn't have a panic attack."

"I noticed." He pressed the cloth to her right knee and looked up at her. "Want to have one now? There's time."

The corner of her mouth lifted, but it didn't stay there long. "When the bullets were coming at us, all I could think about was Emily. I was terrified something bad would happen to her."

"Yeah. I know." Russ had had those same fears. But not just for Emily. For Julia, too. He wouldn't have been able to forgive himself if something worse had happened to her in that parking lot.

"I realized just how important Emily is to me," Julia continued. "And how I would feel if someone took her."

Hell.

Russ knew where this was leading. "Julia, no one

expects you to help with an FBI investigation. Better yet, I don't want you to help. I want you to be safe."

She touched his cheek with her fingertips. "I will be, because you'll be with me."

"Right," he growled, moving her hand away. He recognized that maneuver. She was trying to soothe him. The woman sure learned fast. "You noticed what a good job I did of protecting you today," he mumbled, in disgust.

"Actually, I did notice." Unlike him, there was no sarcasm in her voice. "You shielded me with your own body. You put yourself in the line of fire for me."

Russ wasn't comfortable with her gratitude. He damn well didn't deserve any credit for reacting *after* the danger was right on them. If he'd done things right, if he'd anticipated better, he might have been able to get her out of there before the bullets started.

She caught onto his face again, this time with both hands. "You can't put me ahead of the Richardson baby," she whispered. "And I can't put my fears ahead of him, either."

He stared at her and thought of a lot of things he could say. Russ settled for probably the dumbest one of the bunch. "Who the hell *are* you? Are you the same woman I met in the bar yesterday?"

"I'm Julia Howell, recluse heiress and occasional neurotic. Who the hell are you? Are you the same cocky guy who put his hand up my dress?"

"Absolutely. I haven't changed a bit."

"Liar," she said, and her mouth came to his again.

Unlike the other kiss, there was no desperation in this one. No unspoken need for comfort.

Man, he was a goner.

The air left the room. It left his lungs too, but he didn't need air to feel. One kiss from her, one touch of his tongue to hers, and Russ was already thinking about stripping off her clothes and having sex.

But it couldn't happen.

For one thing, Emily was sleeping just yards away. *Sleeping,* his body reminded him. On the other side of the room. Far away. With her head turned in the opposite direction. Not that she could see them from that far away anyway.

Zoey was in the next room. *The door is locked,* his body reminded him. Besides, Zoey was packing, and he'd told her to stay in her room.

A third argument came to mind—and it was a biggie—Julia was a virgin. If they ever did have sex, it couldn't be something quick and dirty. Well, not the first time anyway.

But the point was, they couldn't have sex right here, right now. Even if his idiot erection had a different take on things.

He started to get up from his kneeling position, but Julia apparently had other ideas, too. It didn't help matters when she moved closer, her knees sliding against his lower chest. Her dress slid too, right up her thighs, but she didn't stop until he was against the bed. And between her legs.

The kiss got hotter. Deeper. He shaped her lips with his, the pressure much harder than he figured it should be. But Russ just kept on, and did his own share of making matters worse when he hooked his arm around and moved her closer still.

With her dress hiked up, it didn't take much effort

for Russ to ease his hand into the back of her panties. Over her bare bottom.

The woman had some curves.

He was playing with fire, but Russ was quickly reaching the point where he didn't care if he burned to death.

He spotted more curves when she leaned down further, and he got a look down her dress. *Mercy.* He fumbled with the tiny buttons on the front and got enough of them undone so he could unclip her bra.

Russ was sure he'd died and gone to heaven when her breasts spilled into his hands.

He looked up at her to make sure she wasn't about to panic, then he rolled his eyes. No panic. Just the face of a hot woman silently saying *take me.* Russ didn't think that was his erection talking, either. Julia was sending out some serious sex vibes.

"We can't," he reminded her. Russ wet his fingers with his mouth and brushed them over her left nipple. She moaned. What a sound. So Russ did it again, just so he could hear her. And then he pleasured both her and himself by taking that already damp nipple into his mouth.

"We can't," she repeated. Her hands raced over him, as if she didn't know what part of him to pull closer, and she wrapped her legs around him.

"I'm not panicking," Julia mumbled, sounding stunned and completely aroused. "I should be. I always do."

"Well, you'd better start panicking soon," Russ countered, "because neither of us is listening to that 'we can't' logic. And we really can't have sex with the baby in the room."

That stopped her. Her breath was gusting, her breasts reacting to those gusts and tempting his mouth with each little movement. Russ had to close his eyes to keep from pulling her back to him.

"You're right," she conceded.

But Russ didn't celebrate the victory of finally getting one of them to back off. It didn't feel like a victory when he could barely walk, but he did manage to get himself off the floor. Once he'd accomplished that, he fixed her bra and buttoned her dress. He then pushed her legs back together so he couldn't see her lacy panties.

"You think this was a danger response?" she asked. "Maybe because we came so close to dying, we needed to feel a human connection?"

Russ wanted to agree with her, but he didn't want to lie. "No. I think we just have the hots for each other. It doesn't make sense. Everything about my investigation is going to hell in a hand basket, and I keep thinking about getting you into bed."

"I keep thinking about that, too," she mumbled.

He gave her a flat response. "That didn't help."

Because this had to end now, Russ took out his phone and went into the sitting room so he could get some updates. He scrolled through his contacts and found the one labeled Pizza Delivery, and he called it.

"Cheesy Jack's Pizza," the man answered. It was Special Agent Chris Soto, the man who'd driven them to the hotel. All the numbers in Russ's phone were coded in case someone like Milo got their hands on it, and the security detail's number had been listed as a pizza place.

"It's me, Russ." He gave them a code word to prove who he was. "Tell me you have good news."

"Some good, some bad. Some very bad."

Russ mentally cursed and tried to brace himself for the "very bad" news.

"No luck getting in touch with Milo," Soto explained, "but the safe house is nearly ready, and we're using a place that's local, just on the edge of town. We just have to put a few more things in place. Oh, and the surveillance disks from the park are on the way over. We don't know if they'll have anything on them, but as soon as they arrive, I'll figure out a way to get them to you."

"Deliver them in a pizza box," Russ suggested. "And what about the shooter?"

Soto's hesitation said it all. Russ groaned. Was this the bad news? "He got away?"

"For now. But we have a description, and we know which direction he was headed when he got into a dark green compact car. The description doesn't match Milo or anyone else who's been involved in this case, so we believe it might have been a hired gun."

That was not what Russ wanted to hear. He wanted the man in custody so they could get some answers.

"Silas lost him," Russ mumbled.

"Maybe." And that was all Soto said for several seconds. "But maybe not. You know that very bad news I mentioned? Well, it's about Silas."

Chapter Nine

Julia sank down onto the foot of the bed to watch and wait as Russ finished his call. She could tell from Russ's side of the conversation that he was talking to a fellow agent. She could also tell that he'd just learned something disturbing. He cursed and stared up at the ceiling for a moment, before coming back into the room with her.

"Silas Durant is missing," Russ told her.

Julia had braced herself for him to say that Silas was dead, that the shooter had killed him; or even worse, that the shooter was on the way to the hotel, but this was news she hadn't expected.

"Missing?" she questioned. "You're sure he's not dead?"

"We're not sure of anything except that he's not answering his phone, and no one has seen him since he went in pursuit of the gunman. No shots were heard after Silas left the park area on foot. An eyewitness saw the gunman drive away and was able to give us a description, but the witness didn't see anyone, including Silas, anywhere near the guy."

Julia shook her head. "Maybe the gunman had a partner? Or Milo took Silas?"

Russ eased down on the bed next to her. "Well, we know Milo wasn't the shooter, so there really wouldn't be a logical reason for Milo to take Silas, even if he'd learned that Silas was a federal agent. If Milo knew that, he'd simply leave. After all, his boss and he have the ultimate bargaining tool—the baby. Kidnapping an agent would be a complication neither would want."

That made sense, but then it still didn't explain why Silas was missing. Russ hadn't completely trusted the man, so therefore, neither had she; but she hoped he wasn't injured, or worse, and was lying somewhere just waiting to be found.

Russ's phone rang again, and Julia immediately glanced at the crib, figuring the sound would wake Emily. The baby stirred but went right back to sleep. Still, Julia got up so she could check on her. It was amazing, but just looking at the little girl could tamp down Julia's nerves. Right now, she needed all the help she could get.

Thanks to the Milo situation—and Russ.

She considered berating herself for the kissing session on the bed. Here she'd hung on to her virginity like some deep, ugly scar that wouldn't fade, and now she seemed more than willing to surrender herself to a man she barely knew.

Except, she did know him. She'd learned a lot about Russ when he'd insisted on raising his dead brother's child. Many men would have just stepped back rather than stepped up. He'd stepped up all right, and was willing to change his life for the baby. She wasn't sure she'd ever met anyone like that.

And she was falling for him.

Julia wanted to dismiss her feelings as pure sexual

attraction, but unfortunately it was deeper than that. Maybe it was their crazy, dangerous circumstances that had created this bond between them. Maybe it was Emily. Either way, the bond was there, and when this investigation was over, Julia was going to have to decide what to do about it.

"The safe house is ready," Russ told her, when he ended the call. "It won't be too far away, so that when this ends, you'll be able to see Emily almost right away."

"But what about Milo's man, the one who was watching the hotel? It won't be safe for Emily to leave if he's still out there."

"He won't be out there much longer. Someone from the San Saba PD is about to arrest him. The charge will be bogus, of course, but it'll get him away from the hotel long enough, and there shouldn't be enough time for Milo to get another man in place."

"Good." That was something, at least. She wanted every possible advantage for Emily.

"The agents are on their way up to get Zoey and Emily," Russ explained. "You, too, if you've changed your mind."

"I haven't changed my mind." Though she wanted to. She didn't want to be away from Emily for even a few hours, much less days. But this was something she had to do.

Russ just stared at her a moment, as if he might try to change her mind, but he didn't. He picked up Emily's diaper bag from the nightstand and began to pack it with the spare diapers and wipes that were next to it.

"You need to get Zoey," Russ let her know.

Julia nodded, gave Emily one last look and went

to Zoey's room. The nanny was already packed and waiting at the door. "Remember," Julia reminded her, "don't tell anyone where you're going."

"I won't. You're not coming with us?"

"No." Julia didn't get into her reasons why. The less Zoey knew about the missing baby, the better. "Just take care of Emily, please, and I'll get to you as soon as I can."

There were tears in Zoey's eyes, probably because the young woman was scared out of her mind. Julia had thoroughly screened Zoey when she'd employed her, and according to the nanny agency, she was supposedly one of the best. But Zoey certainly hadn't counted on the job that included staying at an FBI safe house.

When Julia went back into the bedroom, Russ had already picked up Emily from the crib. The baby was awake, her forehead wrinkled as if objecting to the abrupt end to her nap. Russ kissed both her cheeks, whispered something to her and then passed the baby to Julia. Just as there was a knock at the door.

Julia's heart dropped. She didn't think this was another threat, and she was right. It was the two agents who'd driven them back to the hotel. One was a thin Asian man, and the other was heavily muscled, with blond hair. They were dressed in casual clothes but wore baseball caps with Cheesy Jack's Pizza stamped on them.

One of them handed Russ three large pizza boxes while the other set two thick cardboard carriers filled with cups of soft drinks on the floor. The pair of agents had apparently brought along such a big order to help maintain their cover. It was enough food that it would definitely take two people to deliver it.

"We'll do this fast," the Asian man said. "There's a car waiting at the service entrance at the back of the hotel. There are two decoy cars, too, because we don't want anyone to know which vehicle the baby will be in." He motioned for Zoey to take Emily, and she did, but not before Julia grabbed a quick kiss.

"Keep her safe," Julia whispered to Zoey.

"I will," the nanny promised.

And just like that, before Julia could get another kiss or add anything else, they were out the door and gone.

Russ stood there for several moments with the pizza boxes perched on his left palm, and he blew out a long breath. "The agents are experienced," he told her. "They do this sort of thing all the time. And I trust them."

Those were all the right things to say, but it didn't stop the tears. Julia tried to wipe them away but more came. When Russ spotted them, he locked the door and slid his arm around her.

"I can't believe this," Julia mumbled. "Emily's only been with me two weeks, and I feel as if my heart just walked out that door."

"Yeah." And while the one-word response might have been simple, it was laced with emotion.

Russ gave her a kiss on each cheek, as he'd done with Emily, and tipped his head to the pizza boxes. "You should eat something."

She eyed the boxes. "There's really pizza in there?"

"Smells like it." He set the bottom boxes on the floor and the top one on the coffee table. He opened it. "Cheese, sausage and black olives," he said. "It's probably not your usual breakfast."

No, it wasn't; and she wasn't hungry, despite the fact she hadn't eaten anything for the past eighteen hours. Still, it wouldn't help Emily or the Richardsons' baby if she starved herself. So she got some napkins from the bar area and joined Russ on the sofa. He grabbed a slice, took a huge bite and then lifted the pizza and the foil it was sitting on to extract something beneath.

It was a thick, padded envelope.

"A CD from the park's security system," Russ explained, taking it from the envelope. "This is a copy, and the San Saba PD and the FBI are likely already reviewing it, but I wanted to see if I could spot the shooter myself—or Milo, after he left the meeting."

Yes, she was interested in that, too.

"I need to use your laptop," he said, and headed to the bedroom to get it while Julia ate her pizza. She still wasn't hungry, but her stomach was growling.

Russ ate, too, as he loaded the CD into her laptop and started to go through the images that appeared on the screen. There were apparently multiple cameras, but Russ finally managed to locate the one at the picnic table. He saw Milo, Sylvia, Julia and himself.

He sped up the surveillance, but slowed it again when Milo made his exit from the meeting. Russ adjusted the feed so that it followed the man. Milo took out his phone, made a short call and headed for his vehicle—a black Mercedes that was parked not far from Julia's own vehicle. He drove away.

"You think that call was to alert the shooter?" Julia asked.

"Could be. The lab at Quantico can try to enhance it to see if they can figure out the number he called. We might get lucky."

They watched until Milo was out of surveillance range, then Russ reversed the action on the disk. Next, he changed the camera shots to the one in the area near the trees.

Both of them automatically moved closer, and their arms bumped into each other. Even though they were involved in something that could be critical, Julia wasn't able to ignore the little jolt she felt.

Russ must have felt it, too, because he gave her one of those smiles that made her feel as if she were melting. *Oh, mercy.* She was *so* in trouble.

"Yeah," he whispered. "We'll work all that out later. Promise."

She stiffened. "Am I that easy to read?" she asked, wanting very much to know.

"Sometimes. Don't worry. I don't have you all worked out and understood in my mind. Truth is, you're driving me crazy. I can usually peg people, put them in the right category or box. But I'm not sure where to put you, Julia."

Unfortunately, she understood what he meant. "Maybe the attraction is because of Emily. Because subconsciously we're trying to be parents to her."

Sheez, it sounded worse when said out loud than it had when it was stumbling around in her head. "Or maybe not," she amended.

While volleying glances between the screen and her, he leaned in and gave her a quick kiss. Quick and hot. It was a reminder that the attraction between them had nothing to do with Emily.

However, his smile faded when he spotted something on the screen. "Silas," he said, pointing to the man who was near those trees where the shooter was likely hidden. Silas appeared to be hiding, too.

"He shouldn't have been there," Russ said.

She didn't take the bite of pizza that was already on the way to her mouth. "Where should he have been?"

"Nowhere in the park itself. He was backup, and was assigned to be at one of the park entrances. He certainly shouldn't have put himself in a position where Milo could have seen him. Remember, Silas was supposed to pose as the buyer."

Julia gave that some thought, hoping that it didn't blow the meeting. "So why was he there?"

"I'll ask him as soon as he's found."

A few moments later, the CD showed Silas ducking out of sight. More time passed, and she could see the images of when the shooting started.

Russ panned around, and even though it seemed as if the shots were coming from the trees, Julia couldn't be certain of that.

"Is it possible Silas was the one shooting at us?" she asked.

"I don't know, but he's got some serious explaining to do when he gets back."

If he gets back, Julia silently amended. If Silas was the shooter, if he'd gone rogue, then it was possible the person who'd hired him had already killed him. That could be the real reason he was missing.

Russ's phone rang, and he set aside the rest of his pizza so he could take the call. He glanced at the caller ID, frowned, and when he answered it, he didn't say his name. He only said, "Hello."

"Sylvia," he said, a moment later, and he put the call on speaker.

Good. Because Julia wanted to hear what the woman had to say. It was because of Milo's threat and the shooting that Emily had to be rushed away to a safe house, and Sylvia probably had answers about what was going on. Of course, the question was, would Milo's assistant share those answers?

"How did you get my number?" Russ asked.

"Someone contacted me. A friend of yours, he said. And he wanted me to call you."

Julia hoped that friend was an agent, and she remembered Russ telling the Asian man in the car to try to get in touch with Milo or Sylvia.

"Who tried to kill Julia and me?" Russ demanded.

"We thought you might be able to tell us that," Sylvia countered.

"Why would I know?"

"Because the man who did the shooting was the same person who arrived at the Wainwright Hotel this morning. He went inside and stayed for over a half hour."

She was talking about Silas and the meeting with the Richardsons. It didn't surprise Julia that Milo knew about that, but she wondered how he'd interpreted that meeting. Had he been so suspicious that he'd ordered those shots to be fired?

"What makes you think my visitor had anything to do with the shooting?" Russ wanted to know.

"Because I saw him in the area after you left. Milo saw him, too."

"Maybe because Milo hired him to fire those shots?"

"Impossible," Sylvia insisted. "Milo has no reason to want Julia Howell or you dead. This is simply a business deal, and fired shots and a police investigation would only delay things."

"Does that mean this business deal is still on?" Russ asked.

"It is if you still have a buyer," she replied.

"I do," Russ assured her.

Sylvia didn't respond immediately, and Julia heard someone else talking in the background. "Could you hold on until I step outside?" Sylvia asked. "There's something I need to tell you, and I don't want an audience."

Julia looked at Russ to see if he knew what this was all about, but he only shook his head. They waited for what seemed an eternity, but Sylvia finally came back on the line.

"Look, Milo wants the deal to be completed at noon tomorrow at the city golf course," the woman continued. "He wants both Julia and you there. You provide him proof that the money is in the offshore account, and he'll give you the location of the baby."

"I don't want Julia at the meeting," Russ countered.

"That's not negotiable."

Russ mumbled some profanity. "Everything's negotiable. Just tell him. While you're at it, tell him that he'll only get half the account number for the deposit. And one more thing—I want the meeting to take place here in the lobby of the Wainwright Hotel. No more outdoor venues where people can be in trees to shoot at us."

Sylvia hesitated. "I'll tell Milo what you've requested and I'll get back to you." More hesitation. "Just how much do really know about what's going on here?"

Russ pulled back his shoulders. "What do you mean?"

"I mean we should talk. Face-to-face. Just you, Julia and me."

"Right," Russ mumbled. "Is that because you want a second chance at trying to kill us?"

"I didn't try to kill you!" she practically shouted. "I didn't try to kill anyone." When she continued, her voice was considerably softer. "Look, this is just a job, and I didn't sign up to be an accessory to murder. That's why we have to talk. There's something I have to show you before you walk into that meeting with Milo."

He glanced at Julia and shook his head. "How do I know this isn't some kind of trick?" Russ asked.

"You don't. But I'm willing to meet with you at the police station. I'd be stupid to try to kill you there."

Russ stayed quiet a moment. "Are you a cop?"

"Hardly." Sylvia's answer was fast and loaded with disbelief that he would even suggest it. "I'm just some-one who's concerned about Milo and what's going on. Be at the police station in one hour, and maybe what I show you will help keep us all alive."

Chapter Ten

Russ hoped Sylvia's meeting wasn't a ploy to draw Julia and him out of the hotel. That's why he arranged to have a security detail follow them in the unmarked car that had been delivered to the hotel for him to use.

Still, even with a security detail, there was the possibility that something could go wrong.

Julia was obviously concerned as well, because she kept a white-knuckled grip on the arm rest, and she spent the entire ten-minute drive glancing all around them. Russ wanted to reassure her that they were safe, but he knew that wasn't true. If the person who'd tried to kill them wanted to make another attempt, the only thing that would keep Julia out of harm's way was to send her off to the safe house.

Russ was going to work on that.

He could find an agent to guard her while he had the big meeting with Milo. But if the meeting didn't go as planned for, on the following day with Milo, then he had no choice but to get Julia out of San Saba. Hell, he should get her out immediately, but he was positive she wouldn't go, despite the drained color on her face and her raw, exposed nerves.

"What do you think Sylvia wants to show us?" Julia asked.

"I don't have a clue." And he didn't.

This meeting had come out of the blue, and Russ didn't know if that meant Sylvia was getting cold feet about the deal, or if she had something else in mind. It was that something else that put a knot in Russ's gut. He didn't want Julia in any more danger, but he hadn't wanted to leave her at the hotel either, because no one would go as far as he would to protect her. And it didn't seem to matter if he didn't want to feel that way about her.

"You okay?" he asked her, as they pulled in to the parking lot.

"Don't worry. I'm not about to have a panic attack."

He caught onto her arm and turned her to face him. "That wasn't what I asked. Are you *okay?*"

She moistened her lips, pushed a wisp of hair from her cheek. "I just want this to be over so I can be with Emily."

He wanted the same thing, and he wanted it sooner than later.

Because Russ thought it might help them both, he leaned into her and gave her a quick kiss. It felt comfortable, as if quick, reassuring kisses were part of their normal lives instead of something he'd just started to experience.

"You're not going to put your hand up my dress to stop me from going nuts, are you?" she asked.

Russ thought she was only partly serious, so he kissed her again, and he wished that they were at a place and time where he could figure out where the hell they were going with the dirty thoughts and long, lingering looks.

"Maybe later," he told her, but it wasn't as much of a joke as he wanted it to be.

"Let's get inside," he said. "And make it as fast as you can." The parking lot seemed secure, and there were two uniformed officers milling around outside on what appeared to be a smoke break, but Russ didn't want to take any unnecessary chances.

San Saba wasn't a big city, and neither was the police station. It was a single-story, yellow brick building with a covered walkway across the front.

"I don't see Sylvia," Julia said.

Neither did Russ, and that tightened the knot in his stomach even more.

He'd had his badge delivered with the car, and he stuck it in his back pocket, just in case someone inside questioned him. He locked his weapon in the glove compartment because it would never make it through the metal detector. The trick would be to keep Julia safe and meet with Sylvia without letting her suspect that he was a federal agent.

Julia and he walked past the two smoking officers. Russ made eye contact with him and nodded a greeting before he ushered Julia inside. As expected, there was a metal detector just steps past the door, and they walked through it, thankful they didn't set anything off.

Sylvia was there in the waiting area across from reception. The reception desk was manned by a female uniformed officer, and when she gave him a questioning look, Russ tipped his head to Sylvia.

"I'm here to pick her up," Russ lied.

That seemed to satisfy the officer, and Julia and he

made their way to Sylvia. Russ took the seat directly next to the woman, and Julia sat beside him.

"This had better be worth my time," Russ told her, right off the bat.

"It will be." But Sylvia didn't make a move to show him anything—other than her nerves. The woman's hands were trembling, and her eyes were red—she'd obviously been crying or had somehow faked the look—and she was gripping her purse as if were a lifeline.

"Well?" Russ demanded.

"First of all, I'm in love with Milo, and this meeting is a last resort for me." Her voice was barely audible. "I've tried to reason with him, to talk him out of this deal, but he won't listen. He insists on going through with it, even though I think it's dangerous."

"It *is* dangerous," Russ told her. And he thought about how he should phrase this. "But we can bypass Milo if you know where the baby is."

"I don't." She met his gaze. "But I don't think it's safe for anyone to carry out this deal." Sylvia pulled in a weary breath and opened her purse. "I don't know what's going on, but I hope you can find out."

Julia moved to the edge of her seat, probably so she could see what Sylvia was taking from her purse.

Photos.

She handed them to Russ.

There were two of them, both black-and-white. Grainy shots, obviously taken from a long distance, and perhaps only seconds apart. Two people were in both photos and Russ immediately recognized one of them.

Milo.

Julia's soft gasp let him know that she recognized the other person, as well.

Sylvia stood. "My advice? Before you show up at that meeting tomorrow, you find out why those two are together."

Russ intended to do just that.

Because the second person in the photos was none other than Tracy Richardson, the "stolen" baby's mother.

"I WANT SYLVIA HARTMAN FOLLOWED," Julia heard Russ say to the agent he'd phoned the moment that Sylvia was out of sight. "And have someone call me with the financials on Aaron and Tracy Richardson."

Russ was talking to the agent who'd accompanied them to the police station, and while Julia didn't like the idea of driving to the hotel without backup, she didn't want Sylvia to get away. Not after what the woman had just given them.

She glanced at the photos again before Russ folded them and slid them into his pocket.

"You think they're real?" Julia asked, in a whisper. "Or did Sylvia doctor them?"

"I don't know, but I intend to find out."

Julia only hoped that it was possible before the meeting. She hadn't exactly felt comfortable about going another round with Milo, but this would make things even more questionable. And perhaps more dangerous.

"How long will it take you to get the financial information on the Richardsons?" she asked.

"Not long."

Good, because that might give them some important pieces to this puzzle.

"Is there a place in here to get some coffee?" Russ asked the officer at the reception desk. "Our friend had to run a quick errand, and we need to wait for her to get back," he lied.

She pointed toward a side hall. "It's from a vending machine and tastes like sludge. There's a café across the street if you want something better."

"Sludge is fine," Russ mumbled, and he didn't say anything else until Julia and he were out of earshot. "I want us to hang around here until another security detail arrives."

Julia was thankful for the precaution and equally thankful that the small room with several vending machines was vacant. She had a dozen things she wanted to ask Russ, and she didn't want anyone around to listen in.

While keeping watch around them, he threaded several one-dollar bills into the machine and got them each a cup of coffee. The officer was right. It did taste like sludge.

"So what's going on?" Julia asked. "Why do you think Sylvia really wanted us to meet her?"

"Could be several things." There were four metal chairs lined up across from the machines, and she and Russ sat.

"The pictures could be a hoax. Milo's man could have seen Tracy Richardson at the hotel, followed her and then orchestrated the photos to make it look as if she knows Milo. Heck, Milo and Tracy might have never even met."

"But why doctor the photos to make us think that?"

"Milo could have done it to see how we'd react. This could all be some kind of sick test just to see what we'll do. He might think we'll panic and do something stupid."

Julia couldn't rule that out. "But Tracy could actually know Milo. And that means he could also know that she's the baby's mother."

Russ nodded. "Milo could have figured that out. Or maybe he just suspects she's involved with us. If that's true, it goes without saying that he'll be more suspicious of us."

Yes, he would. And it could be worse than that. "Milo might know you're an agent. Tracy could have told him."

"She could have," Russ readily admitted. "But if she did, I think Milo would have already confronted me about it. He's not shy about saying what's on his mind."

True, but Julia didn't like the possibilities. Sylvia could be playing her own game, maybe so she could turn Russ and her against Milo and then somehow collect the money for herself. Or it could be Milo or Tracy playing a game. A dangerous one.

Russ sipped the coffee and grimaced at the taste. He tossed the cup into the garbage can beside them. "We have to wait and see what all of this means. Maybe Milo wants us off kilter when and if we walk into that meeting. Hell, he might even have Tracy show up so she can get in a bidding war with my *buyer*."

"That's assuming Milo still believes you *have* a buyer," Julia pointed out. "Since Sylvia knew Silas had shown up at the hotel this morning, Milo and she probably also know the Richardsons dropped by for a visit, too. So maybe they now assume that the Richardsons are the ones behind the two-million-dollar offer."

"Entirely possible."

Julia thought of something else. "If Milo knew he could get this much money from the Richardsons, then why didn't he just hold their baby for ransom?"

"Good question, and I don't know the answer. Maybe he thought the buying process would keep him safer, one step away from the authorities. He can definitely control this situation better than he could if he risked going to the birth parents. Hell, maybe there is no actual Z, and *he's* the real seller." He checked his watch and settled deeper into the chair, as if this might be a long wait.

And it just might be.

Even though she grimaced, too, at the coffee taste, she continued to sip it. She needed the caffeine to stay alert, since the fatigue was starting to catch up with her. "You said *if* we walk into the meeting with Milo. I thought we'd gotten past your argument that I shouldn't be there."

"We haven't gotten past it." He leaned his head against the wall and looked at her. "I don't want you there. I want you safe."

"That's your libido talking. You need me there. The Richardsons' baby needs me there."

He blew out an audible breath. "And if something goes wrong? If you're hurt?"

She tried to shrug. "It'd be worth it if the baby was safe."

Russ cursed. "The baby might not be safe because his own mother put him in danger." Since he hadn't exactly said that in a whisper, he looked around to make sure he hadn't drawn any attention. They still had the room to themselves.

"I've been trained to do this kind of thing," Russ said, continuing, his voice quieter but definitely not calmer. "You haven't been. And you shouldn't have to take the risk. I'll just tell Milo that you're sick. Or indisposed. Or that you refused to come. He'll have no choice but to back off about you being there."

Julia wasn't at all sure that would work. Milo was calling the shots, and he could continue to do that as long as he had the baby.

She stared into the cup and wondered if she should even bring this up. The timing was wrong, but then it might not be right for a while. "What are we going to do?" she asked.

"About Emily?" Russ didn't wait for her to answer. "We'll work out an arrangement. Maybe split custody, or something."

"Wow." She took a moment to let that sink in. "You've had a change of heart. Just yesterday, you were reminding me that you were the best choice to raise her."

"I was wrong," he readily admitted. "Emily has to come first. Even if you and I are as different as night and day, we can put our differences aside and do what's best for her."

Julia made a sound of agreement. Partial agreement, anyway. "We're not that different, Russ."

He raised his eyebrows and gave her a dry smile.

She only shrugged. "Maybe our bank accounts are different, but I inherited my money. Not much accomplishment in that. And until I got that call about Emily, I'd closed down. The press called me a recluse. That's a kind word. I would go months without leaving the safe little world I created at my estate."

"But that safe little world *was* safe," he reminded her.

"*Safe* isn't necessarily the way to live your whole life. What about you?" she asked. "Why did you close down and get lost in your job? Does it have something to do with that scar you showed me?"

He rubbed his fingers against it. "Yeah." That was all he said for several moments. He checked his watch again, then his phone. "Three years ago I got sexually involved with a woman in my protective custody." Russ met her eye-to-eye. "She was killed. It was my fault," he added.

"I doubt that."

"Then you're the only one," he mumbled.

So he'd been punishing himself all this time. "You were in love with her?" Julia asked.

"No." There was no hesitation in his answer. "But that didn't make it easier."

"I suspect not. And I suspect you're thinking that this situation with me might be history repeating itself."

"Aren't *you?*" he fired back. "The last time you got involved with a dangerous man, you nearly died."

Yes, and even though there was a huge difference between Russ and her attacker, Julia couldn't completely tamp down the fear. Part of her wanted to take Emily and go running back to her estate; but if she did that, she would never be able to forget the child she could have saved.

Russ's phone rang, and he seemed relieved. Maybe because he wouldn't have to continue this too personal conversation. As usual, he didn't identify himself when he answered, but a moment later she heard him say "Soto."

That grabbed her attention, because he was the agent taking Emily to the safe house.

"They'll be at the location soon," Russ relayed to her.

"Soon? But I thought it wouldn't take them so long to get there?"

"They can't just drive there. They have to make sure no one is following them, so they take what we call a circuitous route. They're doing this by the book. And everything is okay, going just as planned."

Julia released the breath she'd been holding and said a quick prayer of thanks. Emily was away from Milo, and she was safe. Now she had to see what she could do so the Richardson baby was, as well.

Russ stayed on the line, listening to whatever Soto was telling him. He asked about Silas. And about Milo. By the time he ended the call, Julia was anxious for answers.

"What about Silas?" she asked.

"Still no sign of him, but they did locate his phone. It was in a trash bin at the park."

Where he'd last been seen. That could mean Silas had been kidnapped. Or maybe he was setting all of this up so it would appear that way.

Or maybe Silas was dead.

"And Milo?"

Russ shook his head. "He's staying put at his office. He's had no visitors, so if he's been in contact with his boss, then it hasn't been in person."

Russ had no sooner put his phone away when it rang again. Julia hoped this would be the call to tell them that another security detail was in place. She didn't mind being in the police station, but the longer they stayed, the more it might alert Milo that something was wrong.

Again, Julia tried to make sense of what part of the conversation she could hear, but Russ didn't give much away—except for his expression. The muscles in his jaw turned to iron.

"Repeat that," Russ asked the caller.

Julia moved closer and waited.

"I want them brought to the Wainwright Hotel ASAP," Russ insisted. "Keep it quiet, but if they won't come, arrest them. Do whatever you need to do to get them there."

He hung up but continued to stare at the phone. "That was Special Agent Toby Kaplan. He's the one who followed Sylvia. She left here and went straight to another meeting."

"With Milo?" Julia questioned.

"No. With the stolen baby's father, Aaron Richardson."

"What?" Julia was stunned. First, Milo had met with the child's mother, and now Sylvia had met with the father? "Why would Aaron be meeting with Milo's assistant?" Julia asked.

"I don't know, but Toby's bringing the Richardsons to the hotel, and they won't be leaving until they tell us exactly what the hell is going on."

Chapter Eleven

Russ mentally went over the details.

He wanted answers, but he didn't want them at the expense of Julia's safety or blowing the case completely. That's why he'd gotten another room to do the interview with the stolen child's parents. Thankfully, the hotel had very few guests, and other than Julia, none were on the third floor, which was made up entirely of suites. So they'd have privacy, and Russ would better be able to control security.

Of course, nothing was foolproof. But at least this way the Richardsons wouldn't be in Julia's room.

Russ hoped that would be enough.

He had the photos of Tracy's meeting with Milo, and thanks to a fax from Agent Toby Kaplan, Russ now had pictures of Aaron's meeting with Sylvia. It would be interesting to see how the Richardsons reacted when they saw the images. And just in case that reaction turned ugly, Toby would be in the bedroom of the suite, so he could respond.

Of course, the Richardsons could be innocent in all of this. Those photos with Sylvia and Milo could be fake. They could be Milo's attempt at muddying the waters. Or they could be snapshots of desperate parents who'd do anything to get their child back. Still, it was too big of a risk to trust them completely. That desperation could have spurred either Tracy, Aaron or both to cut their own deal with Milo. A deal that involved betraying the FBI and sacrificing Russ and Julia. The Richardsons could have worked things out so they would get the baby, and Milo would get the money—and dibs at killing a federal agent who was trying to bring him down.

The bottom line was that Russ had to be ready for anything.

"It's been nearly an hour," Julia pointed out. She was pacing in the new suite and kept glancing out the window. When she wasn't doing that, she was checking her phone in the hopes that Zoey would call her with an update about Emily.

"They're on their way," Russ answered, though time did seem to be crawling by.

He hadn't realized just how on edge he was, until his phone rang, and he nearly jumped. From the caller ID, he could tell it wasn't Toby, but someone at FBI headquarters. The number was encrypted and listed as unknown. It was yet another precaution, in case he got such a call in front of one of the suspects.

"Yes?" Russ answered.

"It's Denny Lord." Denny was the tech who'd already helped Russ out several times during this investigation. "I have the financials you asked for on the Richardsons. I found a few new things that I didn't find in our initial background check."

Probably because the initial check had been just that—initial. Something to rule them out as obvious suspects in the disappearance of their child.

"The couple has about ten million in assets, mainly from Aaron's trust fund and the business he owns. But I did some checking and found out that Tracy Richardson has some debts in her maiden name. She made some bad investments with her own trust fund and lost nearly everything. I don't think her husband knows about the losses, because he listed her trust as an asset on a recent application for a loan."

"Interesting. What kind of loan?" Russ asked.

"One to make improvements to his business. Or maybe a better word would be to salvage it. He's had some stock market losses, too, and he drained the business profits to cover them."

"Does his wife know?"

"Hard to tell. The loan wasn't made through a bank, but rather, through one of Aaron Richardson's friends who owns an investment company. It's not off the books, but it's not a traditional loan, either. In fact, the money they're using to put up for payment to Milo is from this same source."

So, the Richardsons were having money flow problems and were borrowing to get back their child. That wasn't unreasonable. Unless the Richardsons had actually had their own baby kidnapped so they could play the sympathy card with their money-lending friend. The friend could be in the dark and not have any way of knowing that the payoff money was really a payoff to the Richardsons' debts.

There was a knock at the door. "It's me, Toby," the person said, from the other side.

"Finally," Julia mumbled.

Russ ended the call so he could check the peephole viewer and make sure the agent wasn't being held at gunpoint or something. But everything looked normal for Toby. Not for the Richardsons though. They looked as if they were about to face a firing squad.

Russ opened the door and ushered them in. "Anyone see you?" he asked Toby.

Toby shook his head and lowered his voice so that the others wouldn't be able to hear. "Milo's man is still being held. The guy had an outstanding warrant for writing hot checks. We got lucky."

And luckier still that Milo hadn't sent a replacement. Or maybe he had. Maybe one of the Richardsons was working for him, and that's why Milo hadn't felt it necessary to send in another henchman.

"Sit," Russ instructed the couple. He took out the photos and dropped them on the coffee table in front of them. "And explain these."

Neither Aaron nor Tracy touched them, but they both leaned forward and had a long look. When Tracy saw the one with her husband and Sylvia, her hand flew to her mouth, as if to mask her gasp. Aaron kept his reaction more concealed. He picked up the photo of his wife with Milo and stared at it.

"I met with Sylvia Hartman because I thought she could help me find my son," Aaron offered.

"What made you think that?" Tracy demanded.

Aaron dodged her gaze. "Because I learned that Sylvia works for the man whom I believe has our child. Milo. But obviously, you already know him."

Tracy didn't make another gasp, but it was close. "I can't believe this—"

Aaron held up the picture, cutting off whatever else she'd been about to say. "You didn't tell me about this meeting, either. Why did you see this monster?"

Tracy grabbed the other photo of Aaron and Sylvia and pushed it closer to his face. "The same reason you met with this monster."

"And how did you know they were *monsters?*" Julia asked, taking the words out of Russ's mouth. She wasn't detached from this, either. Judging from the anger in her voice, she didn't think the Richardsons were innocent.

Aaron looked at Tracy. She looked at him. And he shook his head. "The P.I. I hired to follow you also had Milo followed, after he left Julia and you in the alley at the Silver Dollar bar. When he left there, he went to Sylvia, and that's how I learned she worked for him." He glanced at his wife again. "I didn't tell Tracy that part," he explained to Russ.

"Because he knew how I would react," Tracy clarified. "Is Sylvia the woman you've been seeing?"

Russ decided it was a good time to stand there and listen.

"I'm not seeing another woman," Aaron spat out. "I'd never met Sylvia Hartman until I learned she worked for Milo. That's why I went to see her. I thought I could reason with her."

"And you didn't bother to tell me any of this," Tracy fired back at him.

Aaron only waved the photo again, to remind her that she'd done the same with Milo.

"I met with him because I didn't think you were doing enough to save Matthew." She turned her teary eyes toward Julia. "You're a mother. Certainly you understand I was desperate to get back my child."

Julia shook her head. "Desperation I understand.

But you didn't think you were putting Matthew in more danger by meeting with a man like Milo?"

"No," Tracy answered, readily. "I thought I could plead with him or offer him money. But I was wrong. He said he didn't know anything about my son, that I was mistaken, and I should go to the police."

Milo might have indeed said that, because Tracy had already been to the police and still didn't have her son back.

"You offered him money?" Russ wanted to know.

"I did. But he just kept saying he didn't know anything about my son." More tears came, and she buried her face in her hands.

"And you?" Russ said, looking at Aaron. "Did you offer Sylvia money?"

"No. She denied knowing anything about Matthew's kidnapping so I didn't see any reason to offer her anything."

"You should have offered her the money!" Tracy practically shouted. "What, were you trying to save a dollar or two, Aaron? Is that it? You're too cheap to give these people what they want so we can get Matthew back?"

"I want him back." Aaron didn't shout, but there seemed to be a storm brewing behind his dust-gray eyes. "But I'm not convinced either Milo or Sylvia has him. If they did, they would be willing to deal with the source, *with me,* rather than trying to sell him to someone else."

"Maybe this is Milo's way of trying to get a higher price," Russ replied, and Julia nodded. "The longer he waits, the more desperate you become."

"The more desperate *I* become," Tracy mumbled.

"What do you mean by that?" Aaron tossed right back at her.

"It means I don't think you're all that interested in getting our son back."

Aaron didn't answer that—not verbally, anyway. But he silently hurled daggers at his wife. Tracy's tears started to flow again, and Julia crossed the room and caught onto the woman's arm.

"Why don't you come with me," Julia said, softly. "You can freshen up in the bathroom."

Good move. Russ didn't think Julia had freshening up on her mind. Maybe Tracy would spill more with some girl talk. In the meantime, Russ concentrated on Aaron.

"You're having an affair?" he asked Aaron, point-blank.

"No." Aaron paused. "But I've had them in the past. Tracy doesn't trust me."

"Can you blame her?" Russ poured the man a Scotch from the minibar and took it to him.

"She's had affairs, too," Aaron practically whispered, and he downed the drink in one gulp.

Russ sat down next to the man. "Do your former trysts have anything to do with your missing son?"

"No." He didn't hesitate, either. "I think the person who took him is greedy and sick. This is about money, not about my personal life."

"Money and personal lives often cross paths," Russ reminded him.

"Not in this case." Aaron met him eye-to-eye. "I didn't have anything to do with my son's disappearance. I love him, and despite what my wife says, I want him back. I've sold stocks and cashed in investments. I've even borrowed from friends to get the money to pay whatever Milo asks. Would I do that if I didn't love him?"

"I don't know. Would you?" Russ couldn't think of a good reason why he would, unless this was some bizarre way of getting his friends to cough up money.

"I won't continue this conversation without my attorney present." He stood. "I love my wife, too, but I don't think she believes that."

"That might have something to do with your affairs." Russ stood, as well.

Aaron lifted his shoulder. "Those were a long time ago, on my part, anyway. I don't think Tracy can say the same." He paused only long enough to draw a quick breath. "As I said, this interrogation is over, and I'm going to my car. Tell my wife I'll be waiting for her."

Russ didn't stop Aaron when he walked out the door, mainly because he didn't think the man would add more to his story, or change it. Maybe because he was telling the truth.

Or maybe because he'd rehearsed the lies so well that it just sounded that way.

"Do some checking," Russ whispered to Toby, "and see if Aaron told the truth about his affairs being old news. I want to know if he's sleeping with Sylvia."

Toby nodded but didn't say anything, because Julia and Tracy came back into the room. Tracy looked around but didn't seem surprised that her husband wasn't there.

"He's in the car," Russ informed her.

"Of course. Aaron has trouble handling emotional situations. My crying embarrassed him." Tracy turned to Julia. "Thank you for listening."

"Anytime." She gave Tracy a brief hug and walked with the woman to the door. "Remember, call me if you want to talk."

Julia shut the door behind Tracy and waited, no doubt to give the woman some time to get down the hall and completely out of hearing range.

"Will someone follow them?" Julia asked.

"There's an agent posted outside the hotel who'll do that," Russ explained. "I want both of them in our sights until this meeting with Milo is over." He stared at Julia. "So, what did you learn from your chat with Tracy?"

"This isn't exactly a news flash, but the Richardsons are on the verge of a divorce. According to Tracy, she already hired an attorney, and was about to serve Aaron papers when their son went missing."

Russ gave that some thought. If Aaron was telling the truth about loving his wife, then maybe this was his extreme way of trying to hang on to her. It had certainly delayed the divorce.

Toby checked his watch. "I'll get started on the things you wanted me to check," he told Russ. "I have a laptop and some other equipment down in the lobby." Then the agent glanced around. "Should I use this room, or Ms. Howell's suite?"

"This one," Russ decided. If the Richardsons were the real bad guys in all of this, then he didn't want Julia to stay in the suite where the Richardsons had last seen her. It might be an unnecessary precaution, but there was so little he could do right now, that he wanted to take advantage of anything he had.

Russ led Julia back down the hall to her suite, and he made sure no one saw them enter. He locked the doors and turned to see how she was really holding up, but his phone rang.

"It's Soto," he relayed to her.

Russ caught a glimpse of the terror that shot through her eyes. It shot through him, too. Because a call from Agent Soto could be bad news about Emily.

"Is Emily all right?" Russ said, the moment he answered the call.

"She's fine. We're at the safe house. We're only about five miles from you. This is a secure location, with a security system that can monitor the entire area surrounding the house."

"Thanks," Russ told him.

"Don't thank me yet," Soto warned. And Russ braced himself for the news that Soto had obviously not wanted to deliver.

"Is something wrong with Emily?" Julia asked, the moment Russ was off the phone. She had gone pale and had her hand pressed to her heart.

"She's fine. They're at the safe house, and all is well." With Emily, anyway.

Because Julia knew something was wrong, and because she still looked ready to lose it, Russ crossed the room and went to her. "They found the shooter."

She swallowed hard. "And?"

Russ couldn't figure out an easy way to say this, so he just tossed it out there. "He's dead. A single gunshot wound to the head. Could be suicide. Could be an execution."

Her hand dropped away from her chest. "So we don't know who hired him?"

"No."

And they might never learn. A dead man wasn't

going to give them many answers. It didn't mean this was over, either, because the person who'd hired the gunman could turn around and hire someone else.

Russ leaned down a little so he'd be at eye level with Julia. "I don't see any sign of panic."

"Look closer," she mumbled. But she waved him off and scrubbed her hands up and down her arms. "I think I'm past the panic stage, and I've moved on to whatever's next."

"Anger," Russ suggested.

After a moment, she gave a crisp nod. "Yes, I'm angry that I can't be with Emily. I'm angry someone tried to kill us. And I'm also really angry at the possibility that maybe Aaron or Tracy might be responsible for having their child kidnapped. If they're behind this, I want to throttle both of them."

Russ smiled. For a very brief moment, anyway. This new-and-improved version of Julia was going to be trouble. He was a sucker for a damsel in distress, but what really got him revved up was a strong, confident woman. Too bad, because Julia already had him revved up before she'd learned how to cope with the anxiety.

He was about to remind himself why kissing her would be a bad idea, but he gave up. Julia was a lost cause anyway. When this was over, she'd return to her estate and maybe battle with him over the custody arrangement with Emily. She'd probably start dating—someone of her own kind, someone rich, successful and in the old social circle she used to haunt before her attack.

Hell, now *he* was angry. He didn't want her dating anyone else. He didn't want her thinking about any other man. So Russ latched onto the back of her neck and yanked her to him so he could kiss her.

He wasn't sure what he hoped to accomplish. Maybe nothing more than to remind himself of what he'd be missing when this was over.

And he got a reminder all right.

Julia might not have a lot of recent kissing experience, but that little, silky sound of pleasure she made in her throat made up for everything. So did the way she wound her arms around him, slipping her fingers into his hair.

She was the one who deepened the kiss. She was also the one who made it French. But Russ knew he was responsible for upping the stakes when he cupped her breast.

Man, he was out of control.

He should be thinking about the case, but here he was pinching her nipples and wondering if there was enough time to strip that dress off her and taste her the way she deserved to be tasted.

Russ had almost convinced himself to back away, but Julia held on. The kiss just kept on going. So did the touching, and she moved her own hand to his chest to do some touching of her own.

Those chest rubs, and the sex-to-sex body contact, overrode any chance of common sense coming into this. He kissed Julia harder and pushed her against the wall so he could do something about getting her dress undone.

But then he stopped. Pulled back and met her gaze. "Am I being too rough?"

She rolled her eyes, latched onto his hair and pulled him right back to her.

So roughness wasn't an issue. Then what was? Russ decided to do some test touching.

He ran his hand up the back of her thigh, pushing her dress up. She moved into his touch while the searing kiss only got hotter. Hot enough for him to think *to hell with test touching*. He pushed her dress up to her waist and slid his fingers in the direction of her panties.

The scar stopped him.

He felt the raised skin and glanced at it. There was the old wound, right there on her belly.

Julia snagged him by the wrist. "Can we do this with the lights off?"

A loaded question. He was aroused to the point of pain, and part of him was ready to agree to anything— including lights off. But that *"lights off"* was a big red flag he needed to address.

"No," he told her.

Julia blinked. "No?"

"Your scars don't bother me," he let her know. "Well, not like you think. They bother me because of what you went through, but they're reminders you survived. They certainly don't cool this heat that's between us."

She blinked again. And judging from her expression, she probably would have argued, but then he heard a sound. A loud pop.

Before he could react, his phone rang again.

"It's Toby," the caller said, the moment Russ answered. With just those two words, Russ could hear the agent's frantic tone.

"What's wrong?" Russ asked.

There was another of those loud popping noises, and Russ knew it hadn't been caused by a car. He drew his weapon and checked to make sure the door was locked. It was.

"I just got a call from the agent who's been tailing the Richardsons. There's gunfire," Toby explained, his words rushed together. "Just a block up from the hotel."

Russ didn't like the sound of that, or the third shot he heard. "Get down," he told Julia. But she was already headed toward the floor anyway. She pulled her dress back in place and dropped to the thick carpet.

Russ headed to the window. "Are the Richardsons involved?" he asked Toby.

"Not that I've heard. The agent said he followed them to a café, and while he was waiting outside, he saw a man running up the sidewalk with a gun."

Russ glanced out the window but didn't see anyone. "Milo?" he questioned.

"No, the missing agent, Silas Duran. It looks like he's the one firing those shots, and he's coming straight for the hotel."

Chapter Twelve

"Get down here so you can guard Julia," she heard Russ say to the caller.

Julia looked up at Russ so she could try to figure out what was happening, but he was at the window with his back to her. "What's going on?" she asked.

"Silas." And that was all he said for several moments. "He might be the person firing shots."

Silas? So the agent obviously wasn't dead after all. "But why?"

"I don't know."

There was a knock at the door, and Russ hurried across the room so he could peek out through the tiny viewer. A moment later he opened it, and she spotted Toby.

"Toby's going to stay here and guard you," Russ explained.

Julia shook her head. "You're going after Silas?"

"He's my partner. I have to go." That was apparently the only explanation she was going to get, because Russ raced away.

Toby tried to give her a reassuring look, but he failed. Probably because he was standing there, gun drawn, while he kept watching the hall.

"Maybe you should go in the bedroom," he advised. "And lock the door."

That didn't make her feel any safer. "Sweet heaven. You think Silas is on his way here to come after Russ or me?"

"We just don't know. Silas might not even be the one shooting. This is a precaution."

It didn't feel like a precaution. The danger felt as if it were closing in fast. A federal agent had possibly gone berserk, and Russ was out there with him, all because the man was his partner. It sickened her to think that Russ could be facing down bullets while she was tucked away in a hotel room.

Julia stayed crouched down and made her way to the bedroom. She locked the door, as Toby had suggested, and she sank onto the foot of the bed.

She thought of Emily and prayed her little girl was far safer than Julia felt at the moment.

Her little girl, she mentally repeated.

It probably wasn't a good idea to stake an emotional claim on Lissa's daughter, at least not until Julia had worked out the custody arrangements with Russ. Still, she couldn't help it. She couldn't possibly have loved the child any more if Emily were her own, by birth.

She heard another of those loud pops. Another shot, no doubt. And Julia put her hands over her ears to block out the sounds. Without Russ there with her, to anchor her with his wry humor and well-timed touches, she felt the old panic return.

Her heart started to race. Her breathing became thin.

But she forced herself to remember what Russ had threatened to do—to put his hand up her dress.

That gave her a brief reprieve, and made her smile. A smile that quickly faded.

That's because she also thought of the latest kissing session they'd had, a session that seemed to take them one step closer to landing in bed. She wasn't completely certain she was ready for that, but those doubts seemed to evaporate whenever she was in Russ's arms.

Julia lay back on the bed, took the pillows and pressed them against the sides of her head. Finally, it was quiet.

Even though thoughts of Russ were flying at warp speed through her head, Julia focused on her breathing. On staying calm. On slowing her heartbeat. It wouldn't help the situation if she had a full-blown panic attack.

Because she had blocked out the sound, she didn't actually hear anything, but something alerted her. She snapped to a sitting position so she could try to figure out what was going on.

The door burst open.

Her first thought was that it was Russ. It wasn't. The man who'd kicked in the door had dark brown hair.

And a gun.

He shoved something into his back pocket and came right at her.

Julia didn't scream. She couldn't. Her throat clamped shut, and in the back of her mind she wondered if Toby was about to come in and try to save her. But she couldn't wait for Toby to do that. She knew that look in the man's cold, green eyes.

She knew it because she'd seen that look before.

In the eyes on the man who'd tried to kill her twelve years ago.

Julia scrambled across the bed and grabbed the first thing she could reach, the clock. She jerked the cord from the wall and tossed it at the man. It hit his chest, but it didn't stop him. He still came after her.

She knocked the corded phone off the hook, hoping that it would automatically call the front desk or alert someone. Then, she tossed a notepad at her attacker and latched onto the ink pen. It wasn't much against the man's bulky size and his gun, but it was all she had.

She drew the pen back like a knife, and braced herself for him to shoot her.

But he didn't. He came rushing around the bed toward her again. That told her a lot about this situation. He likely hadn't been sent to kill her, but to kidnap her. Or maybe he just wanted to prolong this attack.

Julia stabbed at his beefy arm with the pen and connected, the end of the pen actually scraping into his flesh. He made a sound of pain and paused just a second. That pause was enough for her to try to get to the bathroom. She made it three steps before he latched onto her hair.

The panic returned with a vengeance. Images of the other attack came at her like bullets. The slash of metal on her skin. The pain. The blood.

She felt each stab of the knife again and each inch he'd dragged her over, to the trunk of her car.

This man dragged her, too, toward him, but Julia didn't cooperate with whatever he had in mind. She kicked at him and slapped at him, trying to dig her nails into his wrist. Still, he used his brute strength and pulled her closer and closer. Julia waited until he was right against her, his chest on her back.

She remembered other images, especially those

from her self-defense class. She wasn't helpless, and she wouldn't be a victim again. Julia drew back her elbow, ramming it as hard as she could into his stomach. She didn't stop there. She stomped on his foot, and then pivoted, smacking him in the eyes with the heels of her hands.

He cursed and howled in pain. But he let go of her.

Julia bolted for the bathroom door.

It was open, thank God, and she raced into the small room and slammed the door. Or rather that's what she tried to do. But the man got to her before she could fully close and lock it.

He rammed his heavy weight against the door, and she was no match for his size. Julia flew backwards, her body slamming into the tiled wall between the toilet and the bath.

"You're gonna pay for that," the man growled. He shoved his gun in the back waistband of his pants.

And he came at Julia again.

"STAY INSIDE!" RUSS YELLED to the trio of people in the hotel lobby.

He didn't flash his badge, something he normally would have done, because he didn't want to take the chance that one of Milo's men would see him. He wanted to hang on to his cover, even if there was a chance there was nothing left to hang on to.

Russ stepped through the hotel door, and using the building for protection, he glanced around. There was another shot, and that helped him pinpoint the location of the shooter.

Just to his left.

There was no one on the sidewalks. Thank God.

They'd probably already taken cover or run. Either was fine by him. Russ didn't want an audience, or innocent bystanders getting hurt.

"It's me, Jimmy Marquez," Russ called out, just in case Silas was in earshot. Silas would recognize Russ's undercover name, but the question was—would that cause Silas to shoot? Or would it just give him a direction in which to aim? Because it was entirely possible that Silas was out to kill him.

There was another shot.

This one came from his right, but it hadn't been aimed at the building. Russ crouched down and made his way to the edge of the hotel so he could have a better look.

Another shot.

But this time he saw the gunman—the guy was against the adjacent building and was standing next to a car. It could be Silas. The man was wearing dark pants and a hoodie. And he was indeed armed. Then Russ saw the direction in which the gun was pointed.

His heart went to his knees.

The man had the gun pointed straight up toward the sky. And it wasn't Silas. There was a resemblance, and Russ didn't believe that had been by accident. That's because the shots were a diversion.

Cursing, Russ turned and raced back inside. The shooter would likely get away, but Russ didn't care. Right now, he had to make sure the diversion hadn't been created so that someone could get to Julia.

He jabbed the elevator button, but when it didn't come immediately, he headed for the stairs. He took them two and three at a time. With his heart pounding and a death grip on his gun, he went as fast as he could, because he knew that Julia's life might depend on it.

When he reached the stairwell door of the third floor, he eased it open and looked around to make sure he wasn't about to be ambushed. There was no one lurking around—and that included Toby.

The last time Russ had seen him, the agent had been standing in the doorway of Julia's suite. Russ prayed he'd gone inside.

Russ made his way up the hall toward the suite, and he silently cursed again when he saw the door slightly ajar. Still no sign of Toby, but that all changed when Russ elbowed open the door and saw the agent lying on the floor. Judging from the marks on his neck, someone had used a stun gun on him.

He heard the sounds of the struggle then.

Julia!

He didn't yell out her name, though he had to fight his instincts to do just that. Instead, Russ hurried to the bedroom and took aim.

She wasn't there.

His gaze slashed to the adjoining bathroom, and he heard a loud thump. Maybe a punch. Maybe something much worse.

Russ knew he should try to sneak up on whoever was attacking Julia, but he raced toward the bathroom instead. What he saw confirmed his worst fears.

Julia was on the floor, kicking and struggling. She was trying to break free of the goon looming over her who had a hand locked on her arm. The man reached for something in his back pocket.

A stun gun.

Russ lurched forward and used the butt of his gun to bash the man in the back of his head.

It stopped the guy from getting that stun gun, but he whirled around, and he reached for the handgun that Russ had seen tucked in the back waistband of his pants.

"Please go for it," Russ insisted, though he wasn't sure how he managed to speak. He wanted to kill this guy. Something slow and painful. But he'd settle for a quick kill if he drew that gun. "Give me a reason to put some bullets in you."

The man froze, and Russ's expression must have conveyed that he would have no hesitation pulling the trigger. A moment later, the guy lifted his hands in the air, surrendering.

Russ couldn't see Julia. The room was small, and the big goon was blocking his view, but he did know she was on the floor. And she wasn't moving.

"Julia, are you hurt?" Russ called out to her, without taking his attention off her attacker. Part of him was still hoping her attacker would make one wrong move so this would end right here.

"I'm okay," she said.

But she wasn't. Russ could hear the fear in her voice. "Stay put for just a second," he instructed, and he motioned for the guy to follow him, as he backed out and into the bedroom.

"Facedown on the floor," Russ ordered. "Put your hands on the back of your head." The moment the goon complied, Russ took the guy's weapon and did a quick pat down to make sure there wasn't a backup gun.

Then Russ glanced over his shoulder at Julia. He was scared of what he might see.

She was ghostly pale, as he'd expected, and her chest was pumping as if starved for air. Thankfully, he didn't see any injuries. But mentally, the injuries were there. She had no doubt just relived the attack that had nearly killed her all those years ago.

Julia caught onto the bathtub to steady herself. She got up from the floor, but not easily. Her legs were obviously wobbly, but she finally managed to stand. Russ motioned for her to wait in the bathroom doorway while he called for backup.

Because the guy on the bedroom floor might be wired so that someone, like Milo, could be listening in, Russ didn't identify himself as an agent. He made the call to headquarters and asked for help. Russ had no idea how long it would take someone to respond, especially since the local police were likely tied up with the bogus shooter. He didn't want the locals anyway. This was almost certainly connected to the Richardson baby, and Russ wanted to keep it in-house, if possible.

He thought of Toby and considered having Julia check on the agent, but it was too big a risk. Having the door unlocked was a risk, too. The shooter who had created the diversion could double back to help his comrade.

"Follow me, Julia," Russ told her.

He kept her at his side, with his gun aimed at the attacker on the floor. Once he was in the doorway of the bedroom, he could see Toby. Thankfully, the man was starting to move.

"Lock the door," he told Julia. And Russ kept an eye on her until that was done. She went to Toby to help him. That freed up Russ to get started with the goon he still wanted to kill.

"Who are you?" Russ asked.

When he didn't answer, Russ gave the guy another whack on the head with his gun. "Who are you?" Russ repeated.

"I'll answer questions when the cops get here," he snarled.

"There won't be any cops," Russ informed him.

"Feds, then. Like you."

Russ almost cursed, but he hadn't missed the tinge of doubt in the man's tone.

"What makes you think I'm a fed?"

He made a sound to indicate the answer was obvious. "You were at the police station. I know all the local cops, including the guys they have undercover, and you're not one of them. That means you're probably a fed."

"I'm not a fed. And there won't be anybody coming to arrest you." He jammed his gun against the man's head. "This is between you and me."

Because he was watching him so closely, he saw the sweat pop out on the man's forehead. "You're lying," the guy said.

Since that seemed an open invitation to prove him wrong, Russ whacked the guy upside the head again, and he made sure it was harder than the others. "I'm not lying. And I'm not lying either when I say I'll kill you. After all, you just tried to hurt my woman. I'm not very happy about that, and if you're not willing to give me answers, then I might was well finish you off right now and get to work disposing of your body."

The man angled his eyes at Russ. "You wouldn't."

Russ focused in on the image of Julia fighting for her life against this moron. "Oh yeah, I would."

More sweat popped out on the guy's face, and the seconds crawled by. "All right," he finally mumbled. "I work for Milo."

Of course he did. That also meant Milo must have someone watching the police station after all. That's what had likely prompted this attack. "Tell me something I don't know. Why did Milo send you?"

When the man started to shake his head, Russ rammed the gun even harder against his temple. He winced in pain.

"Milo wanted your woman," the man said, still grimacing.

Russ didn't ease up on the pressure he was delivering to the guy's head. "Why?"

"I don't know. That's the truth," he quickly added, when Russ dug the gun in even deeper. "If you want to know why, then you need to ask Milo."

Good advice.

Russ grabbed the guy's cell phone that was partially sticking out of his pocket. "Call Milo for me," Russ ordered. *"Now."*

Chapter Thirteen

Julia caught onto Toby's arm and helped him to his feet. He was shaky, just as she still was, but he didn't seem injured. He took out his gun and made his way to the bedroom. Julia followed him and spotted Russ crouched down next to the man who'd attacked her. Russ had his gun jammed against the man's head, and Toby took aim at the man as well.

She had an instant of panic when she saw her attacker's face. Hardly more than a flash, before she felt the rage. How dare this monster try to hurt them.

Russ looked back at her, and a dozen unspoken things passed between them. He was worried about her. She was worried about him, too. But he was staying in character, being Jimmy Marquez, the black-market baby broker.

"I'm sorry," Toby told her. And then Russ. "He came at me with a stun gun, and I didn't have time to stop him before he popped me with it."

"Don't worry," Julia assured him. "It wasn't your fault."

Russ nodded, as if to say ditto, but he kept his attention on her attacker. "Bozo here says that Milo sent him," Russ explained to Toby and Julia.

That didn't surprise her, but it did surprise her that the man was frantically pressing in numbers on his cell phone. He then handed the cell to Russ.

"Milo," Russ greeted. "I'd like to know why you sent one of your dogs after Julia."

She wanted to know the same thing, and inched closer. However, Toby nudged her back, probably because he didn't want her too close to the man on the floor.

"Really?" Russ said, with thick sarcasm dripping from his voice. "And you thought the best way to make sure I cooperated with you was to piss me off?" The intense anger merged with his sarcasm.

As upset as Julia was about the attack, she prayed it wouldn't affect the Richardson baby's rescue. In fact, she was even more convinced that Russ and she had to do whatever was necessary to save the child, because Milo was a dangerous man.

"You thought the reason Julia and I were at the police station was because I'm a fed?" Russ questioned.

Julia hoped Russ could convince Milo that it wasn't true.

"Well, you were wrong again. I'm not a fed, and we weren't talking to the police," Russ continued. "We were there because that's where Sylvia asked us to meet her." He paused, obviously listening to what Milo had to say. "Why don't you ask *her* why she wanted to meet us? Are you losing control of your people, Milo? You might want to keep your assistant on a shorter leash."

It was risky, telling Milo about Sylvia, and could ultimately put the woman in danger. On the other hand, this might rid Milo of some suspicions about Russ and

Julia; and after all, Sylvia worked for Milo, so she obviously knew what kind of man he was.

"Julia won't be at the meeting," Russ insisted. "No. That's not negotiable." Another pause. "Fine, then go ahead and get another buyer who'll cough up two million dollars."

Her heart nearly stopped. But Russ just stayed silently on the line.

"I thought you'd see the light," Russ said, a faint smile of celebration shaping his mouth. "Having Julia there would only complicate things."

So she wouldn't be at the meeting. That was good. Well, it was, as long as the deal closed as planned and the Richardson baby was returned.

"No. You're not getting your gunman back," Russ added, a moment later.

The guy on the floor cursed and probably thought he was about to die.

"I'll release him when and if this deal is closed," Russ said. "The meeting happens tomorrow morning, at nine o'clock. Without Julia. Just me, you and the baby. I'll call you with a location. In the meantime, make sure all your hired guns stay far away from me and what's mine."

Russ slapped the phone shut and put it in his pocket—perhaps so he could send it to the FBI for analysis; or maybe he just didn't want her attacker to be able to use it.

Toby went to the man and used the guy's own leather belt to create a hand restraint. He caught onto the back of his shirt and hauled him to his feet. "I'll take care of him. You'll be okay?"

It took Julia a moment to realize Toby was talking to

her. She settled for a nod. No, she wouldn't be okay anytime soon, but she wasn't about to fall apart, either.

Toby led the man out of the suite, and Russ caught onto her arm to lead her out as well. When he pulled the keycard from his pocket, that's when she knew they were going back to the suite where they'd met with the Richardsons.

"We'll be safe there?" she asked.

"As safe as I can make it. Once Toby's taken care of that piece of slime, I'll have him set up a decoy. I want Milo or anyone else watching to think we've left."

"And what about the thermal equipment?"

"The police confiscated it when they picked up Milo's man. They haven't released the equipment, and they won't—not until the FBI clears them to do that."

That didn't mean Milo couldn't use new equipment, but no need to borrow trouble. "Did Silas really fire those shots?"

Russ shook his head. "I don't think so. I believe Milo hired a gunman who looks like Silas to set up a diversion."

She heard the doubt in his explanation. She saw it, too, in his eyes. So Silas might still turn out to be a problem for them.

Russ got her into the suite, shut the door and doublelocked it. He spun around and faced her. "If you want to hit me, go ahead."

Surprised, Julia just stared at him. "Hit you for what?"

"For nearly getting you killed."

Okay. So, that's where this conversation was going. Russ was about to take a guilt trip, and this particular journey wouldn't help either of them.

"Milo did this. Not you," she reminded him. "I'm not hurt, and you got to me in time, before that man could kidnap me."

He shook his head. "It wasn't enough. I've added another nightmare to your dreams."

Hardly. If anything, he'd taken some of those nightmares away. And that's when she realized what she had to do. It wasn't even a tough decision. In fact, it would be a relief on many levels.

Julia went to Russ, pulled him into her arms and kissed him.

RUSS WASN'T EXACTLY SURPRISED by the kiss. If Julia hadn't come to him at that exact moment, he would have been heading in her direction. She just saved them a few steps and moments.

And suddenly every moment seemed to count.

The kiss started hot and hard, and it only got more intense. Russ knew it would, but first he had to give Julia an out. He had to be sure this was what she really wanted, even if it was going to hurt if she put an end to this with just some kisses.

He tore his mouth from hers and looked her straight in the eyes. "This could be about panic. You could be—"

She stopped him with a kiss, and it was a doozie. Julia thrust her body against his, pushing him back against the door. She didn't stop there. She curved her arm around his neck and tightened the embrace.

The need shot through him, consuming him, and Russ figured he only had one more try before both Julia and he were beyond stopping.

He pulled back and held her in place, so that she

couldn't go back for round three. "You don't know me that well—"

"I know you." And she brushed against him and nearly caused his eyes to cross.

Best just to cut to the chase. "Think this through. This is sex, Julia."

She gave a crisp nod. "Good."

Russ groaned. "Sex that you've never had before. And I don't have a condom."

That stopped her all right. She stared at him and blinked. "I'm on the pill to regulate my periods. But I'm pretty sure that covers sex."

"Physically, maybe. But how about emotionally?"

"You want to talk about feelings?" she asked, but she didn't wait for his answer. "Well, here's what I feel. I want you. I've never wanted a man as much as I want you. Now, is that enough for you?"

Hell. It had to be enough, even if he had doubts. There was no way he could turn away from her. Still, sex against the door probably wasn't the way to go here. So he kissed her until she was gasping for breath, scooped her up and headed for the bedroom.

She lit some more fires along the way by kissing his neck and touching his chest. By the time he eased her onto the mattress, he was primed and ready. But Russ forced himself to slow down.

He grabbed both of her wrists in one hand and pinned them to the bed so she couldn't do any more of those maddening caresses. He kissed her again, letting the slow heat slide right through them. It was enough for a moment, but she soon began lifting her hips to meet his.

To hell with slow. It was a lost cause anyway.

Russ unbuttoned her dress and went after her breasts. He already knew how that particular part of her tasted, but he had seconds. And thirds. He kissed every inch of her and then took her right nipple into his mouth.

Julia didn't say anything coherent, and she ground herself against him to let him know what she wanted. *Him.* She wiggled one of her hands out of his grip and pulled up her dress until it was at her waist. She tried to lower his zipper, too, but he was huge and hard, and that didn't make her task easy. Plus, all that groping against his erection wasn't doing much for his willpower.

"Can you cut the foreplay?" she asked, hooking her fingers onto her panties and pulling them off. "I've waited long enough."

Russ couldn't argue with that. Hell, his body would have laughed at him if he'd tried. So he just took what Julia was offering him. Later, he'd deal with the emotional aftermath, and he was pretty sure there'd be one.

He didn't take off his pants, because every second suddenly seemed to matter. Everything was racing. His heart. Julia's caresses. The needy kisses and urgent whispers. He got his jeans unzipped—how he managed that, he didn't know—but it was Julia who took his sex from his shorts.

She guided him to her and lifted her hips. Russ tried to hold back, but she would have no part of gentleness. She wrapped her legs around him and thrust him forward, so that he slid right into her.

There was a flash of pain on her face. Russ cursed and tried to pull out. But she wouldn't have any part of that, either.

"Finish," she insisted.

As if he could have done anything else.

Russ moved inside her, keeping the strokes easy and slow. At first, anyway. Julia soon picked up the pace, and Russ put his hand between their sweat-slick bodies, so he could touch the sensitive flesh at the top of her sex.

He got the reaction he wanted. Julia tossed back her head and dug her fingernails into his back. Russ kept moving. Kept touching. And he watched her face.

Her eyes widened, and her expression said it all. *Ahhh. So that's what all the fuss is about.*

She came in a flash, her body pulling him deeper into hers. The sound of his name repeated on her lips.

She wound her arms and legs tighter around him, and for a moment, Russ got so caught up in watching her that he almost forgot that he was on the receiving end of this, too. Julia's climax was what pulled him back. That, and that look on her face. That look was something he would remember for the rest of his life.

Russ buried his face against her neck and let Julia do the rest.

Chapter Fourteen

Russ was naked right in front of her. He probably didn't know that this, too, was a first for her. She was only an arm's length away from a hot man with no clothes.

How much her life had changed in such a short time. Here, she'd come to this small Texas town to find Emily's father and had also found the man of her dreams.

Well, almost.

Russ was rough around the edges, and perhaps a little dangerous, but he had a way of making her remember that she alive. Like now, for instance.

She idly thumbed one of the iridescent bubbles in her bath. The water was warm and perfect. It soothed what little soreness she had from making love with Russ. And his naked body made her all hot again.

After they'd napped and had eaten the food an agent delivered, Russ had undressed to join her in the large tub, but then he'd gotten a call, an update about the investigation. It was because of that call she'd gotten the nice view of seeing him pace across the bathroom.

He certainly had some interesting parts.

"Yeah, I got that," he said to the caller. He sandwiched the phone between his ear and shoulder while he wrote down something on a piece of paper. He folded the paper and placed it on top of his gun, which was on the vanity.

"Good news," Russ said to her, when he ended the call. "Toby did the decoy departure, so it'll look as if we've left the hotel. I have the number for the account, and the money is in place. We should have the Richardson boy back in…" he checked his watch, "…about twelve hours."

That meant it was around 9:00 p.m. She should be exhausted, what with the adrenaline-spiked day she'd had, and the little sleep the night before, but her body was humming.

"What about the man Toby took away?" she asked.

"He's at the FBI's regional office. Don't worry, he won't be leaving. He'll be charged with a long list of crimes."

Russ frowned, as if he regretted bringing up the attack, so Julia decided to make him forget all about it—something she was trying hard to do. So she smiled and popped more of the bubbles around her breasts so that she could flash him.

Still, it was a paltry effort, considering that Russ was buck naked.

He chuckled, a sound all smoky and thick, and he practically jumped into the tub. The water and the bubbles splashed all over them and the tiled floor. He scooped her up, and she had the pleasure of kissing a soapy, slick, smiling man.

So this was what it was like to have an intimate partner. No wonder people were so anxious to fall in love.

Julia froze at that thought.

Russ noticed, because he pulled back and stared at her. "Everything okay?" he asked.

She wanted to curse herself for ruining the moment. She might not get many of these, and she'd wanted to savor every one.

"Everything's fine," she assured him, and was surprised that it was as true as it had been for her in years. Strange, considering that, hours earlier, someone had tried to kidnap her. Before that, someone had fired shots at her. Yet, here she was, panic free.

And aroused.

She leaned in and took pleasure in a long, slow taste of Russ's mouth. A taste cut way too short because Russ's phone rang.

He cursed but got up from the water, the suds streaming off his rock-hard body. Julia knew he couldn't just ignore the call, because it might be related to the investigation, but she hoped it wouldn't take him too long to handle whatever it was.

Russ grabbed a towel, wound it around his waist and grabbed his phone. He glanced at the screen and frowned.

"Yes?" Russ said. A moment later, he added, "Silas?"

That grabbed her attention, and Julia sat up so she could listen. Thankfully, Russ put it on speaker while he dried off.

"Someone tried to kill me," Silas insisted. His words were rushed, and his voice was anxious.

"Where are you?" Russ ignored the bombshell Silas had just delivered.

"I'm here, at the service entrance to the hotel. Russ, you have to let me in."

Sweet heaven, Julia thought. *What else could go wrong?* But she immediately rethought that. Silas might not be telling the truth. Obviously, Russ had his doubts, too. After all, the man had gone missing only minutes after someone had fired those shots in the park, and Silas was implicated again in the ruse shooting.

"What hotel?" Russ questioned.

"The Wainwright, of course, where Julia and you are staying."

Russ's jaw tightened. "Who says we're still there?"

"I paid one of the maids to check. I paid her to use her phone, too, because I lost mine when I was chasing the shooter at the park. You have to let me in, Russ. I'm hurt, and I need some help."

"Hurt how?" Russ asked.

Russ continued to dry off and then reached for his clothes. Since Russ might have to leave the room to help Silas, Julia got out of the tub so she could dress as well. So much for her humming body and those extra kisses she'd been anticipating.

"I can't get into that now," Silas insisted. "Didn't you hear me? Someone tried to kill me."

"I heard. The problem is, I'm not sure I believe you."

"What?" Silas howled. "But you have to believe me. I'm your partner, Russ."

Russ groaned. He was obviously torn between whether he should help Silas or not. "I know who you say you are." Russ let that hang between them for several seconds. "What happened to you? Why did you disappear from the park?"

Silas cursed. "I was in pursuit of the shooter when someone came up from behind me and hit me with a stun gun. I lost consciousness, and when I came to, I was tied up in the backseat of a car. The driver took me out into the sticks and dumped me."

Russ pulled on his jeans and zipped them. He also stuffed the folded piece of paper in his front pocket. "Describe the guy."

"Dark brown hair. Green eyes." Silas didn't hesitate, and Julia immediately realized that was a similar description to the man who'd attacked her.

Still, it didn't mean Silas was innocent. Maybe her attacker and Silas were working together.

"You have to let me in," Silas repeated.

Russ shook his head and finished dressing. "No, I don't. And I won't. I can't risk putting Julia in any more danger. Besides, we're not at the Wainwright. The maid you paid off was mistaken."

"Julia?" Silas spat out. "You won't help me because of her? You're putting her ahead of me?"

"Absolutely," Russ said, not hesitating. "I know she's innocent, but I'm not so sure about you. And until I'm sure, here's what I want you to do. Call Toby."

"I don't have his number. Hell, I don't have anyone's number, because I'm not using my own phone. Yours was the only number I remembered. That's why I called you. That, and because I was sure you'd help."

Russ's jaw muscles continued to stir, and he rattled off some numbers to Silas. "That's Toby's cell. Tell him where you are and he'll come and get you immediately. He won't be alone," Russ warned.

"So Toby suspects me, too?" Silas asked. In addition to the anxiety, now there was anger.

"It's just a precaution," Russ explained. "If you're

innocent, then I'll owe you a huge apology." He paused. "How bad are you hurt?"

"I'll live." Silas mumbled something she couldn't understand, but it was clear that the man wasn't happy about Russ's decision. "It's just a broken arm. It happened when my kidnapper dumped me from the car."

"Any idea why the guy didn't just kill you?" Russ asked.

Silas hesitated. "I don't know. Maybe he kept me alive so I'd look guilty. But I'm not."

"I hope you're right. Call Toby," Russ told him, and he gave Silas the number again before he hung up.

"Could Silas be telling the truth?" Julia immediately asked. She hurriedly put on her dress and finger-combed her wet hair.

"I hope to hell he is. But I don't like that he's here at the hotel. At the very least, it's suspicious. But it could be far worse than that. We need to leave."

That sent her heart racing. "Right now? With Silas still nearby? Remember, you tried to convince him that we were at another hotel. If we try to leave, he might see us."

"We won't leave until I'm sure Silas has contacted Toby." Russ shoved his gun into the slide holster of his jeans. "We'll give Toby a couple of minutes to respond, and once he has Silas away from here and on the way to the hospital, then we'll use the unmarked car in the parking lot to leave."

Julia thought through all those steps they'd have to take. "Will we be safe?"

He looked at her and planted a quick kiss on her lips. "Safer than we will be here. I don't think Silas believed we were anywhere other than at the Wainwright. And if Silas is working for Milo, then this could be the start of another attempt to kidnap you."

That made the danger crystal clear. Milo could still want to use her as leverage, so that Russ would fully cooperate at the meeting. She would be Milo's insurance policy. And his hostage.

Julia nodded and slipped into her shoes. "Just let me grab my purse and we can go."

With Russ right behind her, Julia hurried to the bedroom, but she only took a few steps, when the lights went out, plunging the room into total darkness.

RUSS DREW HIS GUN, because he didn't believe this was a coincidence. Only a few minutes after he'd refused to help Silas, the power had gone out in the hotel. Either Silas was responsible, or Milo just wanted to make the agent look guilty. There wasn't time to figure out which.

Russ took out his phone. Thank God for the backlit keypad, because his eyes hadn't had time to adjust to the darkness. The drapes were all closed, and it was possible the street lights would help illuminate the room; but he didn't want to take the risk of someone watching for him to open the curtains.

He pressed in Toby's number, and waited.

Toby didn't answer. On the seventh ring, Russ gave up and slapped his phone shut. This couldn't be good. Even if Toby was helping a wounded Silas, the man still should have been able to answer his phone. Unless someone—or something—was preventing Toby from answering.

"What do we do?" Julia asked.

Her breathing was already too fast, so Russ pulled

her to him. He couldn't take long to comfort her, because he had to call headquarters for backup.

The sound stopped him. Someone was pounding on several of the doors. Russ didn't answer. He put his fingers to Julia's lips so she'd stay quiet, as well. But he was praying it was Toby out in the hall.

"It's me," someone called out. "The lights went out when I was coming up the stairs. I can't see my hand in front of my face out here."

Not Toby.

Silas.

"Russ, if you're in one of these suites, you have to let me in," Silas demanded. "Toby didn't answer his phone, and I've got no way to protect myself. And we have to protect ourselves. There's some guy in the parking lot, and I'm sure he's got some thermal imaging equipment. I think he's looking for us."

Oh, man. That wasn't something he wanted to hear. "Don't answer him," Russ whispered to Julia.

Silas knocked again, and it sounded as if he were at the door across the hall from them. "Russ, are you in there? The maid told me you were probably in one of the suites on this floor. I'm in pain, and I need help. *Please.*"

Russ waited, his breath held. Beside him, Julia did the same. He hated not responding, but he couldn't take the risk. He only hoped Silas would understand, if he turned out to be innocent in all of this.

Silas moved to their door, and he started to hit his fists against it. Russ hoped the locks wouldn't give way. Just in case, he aimed his gun in that direction. He wasn't happy about the possibility of having to shoot a fellow agent, but if Silas came through that door, Russ couldn't let him get to Julia.

"I'm going to the front desk to ask them to call for an ambulance," Silas said, his voice way too loud. Even if he was completely innocent, he had to be drawing some attention. The wrong attention, no doubt.

The pounding and shouting stopped. Russ waited, listening, and stayed quiet. He wanted to call head-quarters, but Silas was possibly still lurking outside the door.

He brushed his fingers along Julia's arm again and hoped it would keep her calm. This had to be scaring her to death. It was scaring him, too, and he hoped he could get her safely out of there.

The seconds crawled by, each one ticking off in his head. Russ thought of Toby, of reasons why the man wouldn't be answering his phone, but none of those reasons were good. Maybe, just maybe, Toby was still alive.

Russ took out his phone again to call headquarters. It wasn't his first choice of ways to handle this incident, because if agents had to come into the hotel for a full scale rescue, it might blow his cover. That couldn't happen with him so close to getting the Richardsons' baby back.

Russ had barely opened his phone when he heard the sound.

A crash.

Russ automatically pushed Julia to the floor, and he crawled over her to protect her with his own body. He glanced around, trying to pick through the darkness to see what had happened. The door was still closed, so Silas, or someone, hadn't broken through it.

He spotted the glass then. Shards of it glistened on the floor. And Russ knew why. There was a hole in the drapes, and light from the outside was pouring through the tiny opening.

What the hell had happened? But he soon knew.

There was another crash, more of a soft pop, followed by the sound of breaking glass. And that's when Russ realized that someone was shooting at them with a gun rigged with a silencer.

Chapter Fifteen

Julia felt something smack into her leg, and she glanced behind her to see what it was. A shard of glass. Something had broken through the window and sent the glass flying.

Was someone shooting at them again?

If so, there hadn't been a loud bang like the shots in the park, or the ones fired earlier, outside the hotel.

"Let's go into the bathroom," Russ told her. He helped her get into a crouching position so they could get moving. But there was another swooshing sound.

The bullet, or whatever it was, tore through the thick drapes and sent more glass onto the floor.

That got Russ moving even faster. He practically pushed her to the floor and took out his phone. She waited and prayed, while he called for backup, but he only cursed.

"Someone's jammed the lines," Russ told her.

Her heart dropped. *No. This couldn't be happening.*

"Go into the bathroom," he said.

There were no windows in that room, so Julia was about to run in that direction, but the next sound was considerably louder than the others.

Not a bullet coming through glass.

This was much louder and more of a crashing sound. Light rushed through the sitting room, spraying out from the window, and she soon knew why.

Someone had actually broken through the window.

But how? They were on the top floor of the three-story hotel. That meant that someone had gotten to the roof and climbed out onto the ledge outside the window. It wouldn't have been difficult to do.

"Get down!" Russ shouted to her.

Julia dropped to the floor, and it wasn't a second too soon. One of those silenced shots came flying into the bedroom. Not at Russ, but at her.

The bullet slammed into the thick down comforter and sent feathers swirling around like confetti.

Russ returned fire. Unlike their attacker, his shot wasn't muffled through a silencer. It was a loud blast that echoed in the room.

She caught a glimpse of the shooter diving to the side of the sofa. Russ took cover, as well, behind the slightly ajar bedroom door. But Julia knew that wouldn't be much protection. Bullets could easily go through wood.

Julia wanted to yell for Russ to slam the door and get down, but she couldn't risk giving away their exact locations. Especially hers. The gunman had fired at her.

Why?

Earlier, Milo had tried to kidnap her, but now it appeared that Milo, or someone else, didn't care if she was killed. Did that mean they no longer needed her for leverage, or did this have something to do with Silas?

Another shot came her way and hit the pillows that were stacked against the headboard. Julia flattened her body on the floor and covered her head.

She considered trying to get into the bathroom, but it was too dangerous for her to move now. There was more than enough light coming from the broken windows for their attacker to see them and take aim right at her.

The next shot tore into the nightstand, just inches above her. She heard Russ curse, and he came out of cover with his gun pointed.

"No!" she shouted. He could be killed, and all because he was protecting her.

But that didn't stop him. Russ fired a shot, then another.

The next sound she heard was something or someone falling to the floor. A loud thud, like deadweight crashing against the carpet.

For a moment Julia lost sight of Russ, and that sent her into a near panic. He wasn't be hurt. That sound couldn't have been him falling.

But then she heard footsteps and followed their sound. Russ was still there. Standing. And he didn't appear to be injured. He had his weapon and was inching into the sitting room.

"Is he dead?" she asked.

Russ didn't answer. She saw him shake his head, and he disappeared into the other room.

Julia started praying. She hated that she wished someone dead, but better their attacker than Russ or her.

She forced herself to slow her breathing. Not easy to do. But she formed an image of Russ and Emily in her mind. She didn't let that image waver, and she drew much needed strength from it. She had to get through this for them. Emily needed her, and Russ would go through a bad guilt trip if she went crazy on him.

"He's dead," she heard Russ say.

The relief was immediate, and she jumped to her feet so she could see for herself. But Russ was there in the doorway, and he turned her away from the dead man.

"He has a thermal monitor on him," Russ explained. "This is the guy that Silas saw in the parking lot."

No doubt. And he'd used that equipment to pinpoint them for an attack.

"My phone isn't working," Russ added. "But someone probably heard those shots. I'm thinking we'll wait here until the cops arrive."

Julia nodded, and then went willingly when he pulled her into his arms.

"Why did he want me dead?" she managed to ask. "It doesn't make sense. Milo probably thinks I'm the buyer. He likely believes I'm the one who'll be giving him access to the money. So why would he risk killing me?"

"I don't know." Russ brushed a kiss on her cheek. "But I intend to find out."

Yes, but that would take time. "What about tomorrow morning's meeting?"

"I'll go with backup," he said.

Backup suddenly didn't seem nearly enough. Still, what other choice did Russ have? They couldn't let the Richardson baby be sold to someone else.

She stood there in his arms, while she listened for the sound of sirens. But she didn't hear any. Maybe because it was too soon. Maybe the cops were on the way but still out of earshot. She didn't want to think of the alternative—that Russ's bullets had been dismissed as a car backfiring.

"How long do we wait?" she whispered.

"As long as it takes."

But the words had no sooner left Russ's mouth when Julia finally heard something. It wasn't what she wanted to hear.

It was coming from the hallway.

There was another of those deadly swishing sounds. And this time, she knew exactly what it was.

Someone had fired a shot just outside their suite.

NOT AGAIN.

That was Russ's first thought, quickly followed by a trained response that he had to do something, anything, to protect Julia. For whatever reason, someone was out to kill her tonight.

The dead guy on the floor had certainly tried. And failed, thank God. Russ had wanted to find out who he was, and better yet, who had sent him. But those questions would obviously have to wait.

Round two had begun.

There was another shot in the hall. It also came from a gun rigged with a silencer.

Apparently, someone didn't want to be detected. Too bad Russ couldn't just start firing shots at the ceiling, so that it would alert someone to call the police, but he couldn't waste the ammunition. He didn't have any extra magazines with him, or a backup weapon. Since he was using a smaller, more compact handgun, suited for undercover work, he'd only started with fifteen rounds—two of which he'd spent on the dead guy.

Thirteen better turn out to be a lucky number,

because that wouldn't be enough firepower if he got into a long gunfight.

Russ caught onto Julia's arm and positioned her behind the bar. It wasn't an ideal location, since it wasn't that far from the now gaping window where the gunman had entered. But the bathroom was out, since it was on the same side of the wall as the hall. In fact, that could have been where the last shot went. Anyone with any experience in attacks would have known that Russ would have sent Julia into the bathroom.

And he'd nearly succeeded in getting her there. But blind luck again had kept her remaining safe. Later, he'd kick himself for not getting her out of town. She should be at the safe house with Emily. But instead she'd stayed behind, and was now in danger because of it.

Russ stayed in front of her and tried to keep watch on all sides. If someone tried to break down the door, he'd have time to fire, but he couldn't cover both the door and the window. If the assault came from both sides, they were in trouble.

There was another shot. And it confirmed what Russ had already suspected. Someone had fired into the bathroom. This wasn't just an ordinary attack. It was a mission of murder.

Now the question was why?

He checked his phone again: still blocked. He picked up the house phone, but it was dead as well. Though maybe, just maybe, help was on the way.

Just in case this turned ugly, Russ took the folded piece of paper from his front pocket and stuffed it in between the foil-bagged nuts on the bar. Leaving it there was a gamble, but it would be an even bigger gamble to keep it on him.

There was a thump at the door. Not exactly the sound of a kick, but close. Russ aimed his gun in that direction and braced himself for another attack.

He didn't have to wait long.

The second attempt was a hard kick to the door. The locks held. Until the person fired a shot into the lock. Not one, but three. Each rough gust was followed by the sound of metal slashing through metal.

Russ's heart was in his throat, and he had no doubt that Julia was about to lose it. She didn't have his training. But she damn sure had the experience with violent situations. This was no doubt causing an avalanche of flashbacks.

"Stay down," Russ warned her, in a whisper.

Another bullet went into the lock, and it was followed by a hard kick. Russ got ready. His finger tightened on the trigger, and he tried to get the best aim he could. He had no idea who or what was coming through the door, but he might have only one shot to save Julia.

The door burst open, and Russ was within a split-second of firing when he saw the man's face.

Silas.

But he wasn't armed, and he didn't look as if he had the strength to kick down a door. There was blood on his forehead and on the sleeve of his shirt. He was holding on to his left arm.

"I'm sorry," Silas said. He hadn't said it clearly, either. He slurred the two words.

Russ wanted to ask "sorry for what?" But he soon realized Silas wasn't alone.

Someone was standing directly behind him.

Russ couldn't see the person's other face, but he had no trouble seeing that a gun was aimed at Silas's head.

That put a knot in Russ's stomach. He hadn't trusted Silas when he'd called out earlier, and maybe because of that lack of trust, Silas was now in danger. Still, Russ hadn't had a choice. The agent's behavior had been too erratic for Russ to believe him and let him anywhere near Julia.

"I depended on the wrong person," Silas mumbled, and that remark caused the individual behind him to jam the gun harder against his head.

Russ pushed aside Silas's comment. Later, there'd be time to question his partner as to what he meant by that. Right now, Russ had to deal with what was essentially a hostage situation. And Julia was right in the middle of all this.

"Who are you?" Russ demanded of the gunman. He kept his gun aimed, but he knew he couldn't fire. Silas was literally a human shield.

The person didn't answer for several seconds. "It's me."

Russ had no trouble recognizing that voice. It was Milo.

Apparently, Julia recognized his voice, too, because she made a soft groan.

This latest incident shouldn't have surprised Russ— he knew the man was a criminal—but what he couldn't figure out was why this was happening. The meeting had been scheduled. He had the number for the offshore account. Within a matter of hours, the baby deal would have been closed, and in theory, Milo would have a lot of money for his part in the illegal transaction.

So what had happened to make Milo resort to this?

Maybe Milo had objected to Russ's insistence that Julia not be at the meeting. Or maybe he had just gotten suspicious. Something had certainly set him off, if he was holding a hostage at gunpoint.

"What do you want?" Russ demanded.

Again, Milo took his time answering. Russ shifted a little so he could see him, and Milo was glancing all around the hall, as if he expected someone to jump out and attack him.

Good. That probably meant Milo didn't have backup, either. Maybe because his backup was supposed to have been the dead guy now lying on the floor.

"I want Julia," Milo finally answered.

Everything inside Russ went still. Hell. He didn't hear any reaction from Julia. He didn't have to. Russ knew she had to be terrified at the thought of being held captive by this monster.

"Why do you want Julia?" Russ asked the man.

"Because if I have her, then I can make sure you cooperate."

That didn't make sense. "You already had my cooperation before you decided to pull this stunt."

"No. I had the façade of your cooperation. I know who you are, Special Agent Russ Gentry. And I know this is a sting operation to bring me down."

Russ tried not to react to that. He had to stay calm. And he prayed Silas did the same. The agent was sweating like crazy, and he was grimacing in pain.

"If you believe I'm an agent out to get you, then why do you want Julia?" Russ wanted to know.

"Because I still need the money, and I can be sure that you'll give it to me if I have her."

Russ chose his words carefully. "The deal can still happen. You give me the baby, and I'll give you the number for the offshore account."

Milo laughed. "Not without some insurance. Julia is that insurance."

Milo was obviously lying. Just a few minutes ago, the dead gunman had tried to kill her. And then someone, probably Milo, had fired shots into the bathroom, the most likely place for her to be. This was more than just Milo wanting some kind of insurance. He wanted Julia dead.

Why?

The reason didn't matter; Russ wasn't going to let Milo get the chance.

"You don't want Julia," Russ tried again. "Make a call. Get the baby here, and I'll give you the number of the offshore account so you can get that money. Everybody will be happy, and no one else gets killed."

"No," Milo answered.

"No to which part?" Russ asked, holding his breath. This couldn't fall apart now.

"To all of it," Milo calmly said. "If Julia doesn't come with me, there'll be no exchange. And you won't get your hands on the baby. In fact, if I don't make a call within fifteen minutes, the baby will be taken out of the country, and neither his parents nor you will ever see him again."

Russ took a deep breath and got ready to go another round with Milo. He had to make this deal happen. But before he could say anything else, he heard movement behind him. He also saw Silas shaking his head. It didn't last long, because Silas's eyelids fluttered down, and the man appeared to lose consciousness. At least Russ hoped that was all it was. It was possible that he was close to death, because Russ had no idea how serious his injuries were.

Despite Silas going limp, Milo hung on to him and continued to use him like a shield.

"I'll go with you, Milo," Russ heard Julia say.

Despite the fact that he wouldn't take his eyes off Milo and Silas, her words caused Russ to look at Julia. She had her hands lifted in the air.

Surrendering.

Russ cursed. "Get back," he ordered.

"No," she answered. Her voice wasn't nearly as calm and assured as Milo's, but that didn't stop her from moving away from the bar, and closer to Milo.

She looked at Russ, and he saw the determination in her eyes. "I'm not going to lose the baby," she insisted.

"Smart woman," Milo proclaimed.

Russ wanted to shoot Milo for encouraging her and putting her in this position. "This isn't smart," Russ told her. "He wants to kill you."

But that didn't stop Julia.

Russ tried to latch onto her and pull her back, but she walked straight toward Milo.

Chapter Sixteen

Julia forced herself not to think beyond the moment. She didn't want to put herself in harm's way, but she also didn't want the Richardson baby to be taken out of the country.

She thought of her own precious Emily—of how horrible it would be to have her stolen from her, never to be seen again.

Julia also thought of Russ. He definitely didn't approve of what she was doing. He was the protector, and he wanted her safe.

But sometimes being safe wasn't the right thing to do.

Russ reached out to grab her again, but that caused Milo to dig the barrel of his gun into Silas's head. "You want him dead?" Milo taunted. "Because that's what will happen if you don't stop."

Julia glanced at Russ and tried to reassure him that this was the only option they had, but he only shook his head and demanded that she back up.

She didn't. When she was within just a foot or so of Milo, he shoved Silas forward, nearly pushing him straight into Julia. When she stepped to the side to avoid the impact, Milo latched onto her and pulled her in front of him.

Now *she* was Milo's hostage.

"Let her go," Russ demanded. He glanced at Silas, probably to make sure the man was okay, but then he nailed his attention on Milo and Julia.

"See?" Milo said in a sappy sweet, mocking tone. "You're already in a more cooperative mood. No more demands from you. No more lies."

Russ's eyes narrowed, and the muscles in his jaw went stiff. "What do you want?"

"The number of the offshore account."

Julia had expected him to say that, and she also expected Russ to start bargaining. She didn't have to wait long.

"I only have half the numbers," Russ told him. Julia knew that was a lie. "The other half is with the buyer."

"Then you'd better get those numbers now or I'll kill Julia," Milo insisted.

Russ lifted his shoulder. "Julia's my ex-lover. Nothing more. She doesn't mean anything to me."

Julia knew this was a ploy, but she couldn't believe how convincing Russ was. Or how much it hurt to hear him say that. He certainly meant a lot to her. Too much, maybe.

She was in love with him.

It wasn't the best time for her heart to announce that to her head, so she pushed it aside. Later—if there *was* a later—she would deal with her feelings. Right now, she had to stay alive and stop Milo from hurting anyone else, especially Russ and the baby.

"Just your ex-lover, huh?" Milo asked. "You don't expect me to believe that."

"It's true," Russ fired back.

Because Milo's chest was against her back, Julia felt Milo go stiff. His tone might be all calm and cool, but he was getting agitated. He had counted on Russ being willing to do anything to protect her. Maybe that's what the shots had been about. If one of those bullets had seriously injured her, Russ would have handed over the account numbers to save her life. And in doing so, Milo would have likely killed them both.

From the corners of her eyes, Julia looked down the hall, in case she needed an escape route. It was dark because the electricity was still off, but there was a window at the opposite end of the suite entrance, and some light trickled in. Enough for her to see that there was no one else around.

But the door immediately next to her suite was ajar.

Mercy. Russ had already told her that there weren't any other guests staying on the third floor, that the all-suites floor didn't get much use at the Wainwright, but that didn't mean someone couldn't have sneaked up there. She hoped Milo didn't have one of his hired guns in there, waiting to step in and help.

"Here's what happens now," Milo said. The calmness faded. "You give me *all* the numbers of the offshore account number, and once I've verified that the money's there, I'll take Julia out to the parking lot, where I'll give her the baby."

Julia wanted that to be true, but she knew she couldn't trust him. Once Milo had the full account number, there was no reason to keep any of them alive.

Russ didn't look at her. He kept his attention trained on Milo. "The buyer won't give me the other half of the account until I have proof that we have the baby."

"Then we're at a stalemate," Milo said, his voice a threat now. "You'd better hope my finger doesn't tense, or the bullet will go right into Julia. And despite what you said about her being your ex-lover, I'm betting you still feel enough for her that you can't let her die this way."

Russ didn't flinch. Didn't react. But Julia had to bite her lip to keep from making a sound.

"A stalemate's not going to do either of us any good," Russ said.

"You got a better idea?" Milo asked.

"I think I do. You and I can go to the parking lot together. Just the two of us. And after we both put down our guns, I can call the buyer for the second half of the account at the exact moment that you put the baby in my arms."

She braced herself for Milo to laugh or say an outright *no,* but he didn't.

"All right," Milo agreed. "But we keep the guns. For now. And Julia goes with us."

"No," Russ barked, angrily disagreeing. "She'd only be in the way."

"Maybe she'll be in *your* way, but not mine. I'd prefer not to be shot by a sniper when I walk out of this hotel."

Julia waited, holding her breath. She held it for so long that her lungs began to ache.

Russ finally nodded. "Let's finish this."

Julia didn't feel any relief. They still had a long way to go, and too many things could go wrong. But maybe this was a start. Still, she had to be ready to escape, because all of this could be a trick.

Milo moved slightly, so he could turn her to face the hall. "You first," he told Russ.

Russ hesitated. "We go side-by-side," he insisted.

Probably because he was concerned that Milo would shoot him in the back. And he just might try to do that. But Julia figured Russ was safe, at least until Milo got those account numbers he wanted.

With his gun still aimed and ready, Russ mumbled something to Silas, and he stepped out into the hall with Milo and Julia. She was ahead of them, but glanced over her shoulder at Russ.

Julia tried to read what was going on in his mind, but then Milo pushed her forward to get her into position. She adjusted her stance, and Milo curved his left arm around her throat so that she wouldn't be able to get too far ahead of him. And so he could keep his gun pressed to her head.

Russ stayed on Milo's right, and together the three of them started up the hall.

They'd only made it a few steps when Julia saw the movement. It'd come from the room next to her suite.

The room with the open door.

Julia started to call out to Russ, to warn him, but it was already too late.

RUSS SAW THE FLASH of movement to his right.

He automatically pulled back and turned his weapon in that direction, but he found himself gun-to-gun with the person just inside the dark doorway.

"Shoot and Julia dies," Milo reminded Russ.

Russ held back on pulling the trigger, and he tried to

focus on the person across from him. Unfortunately, the light wasn't cooperating. He could see some things in the hall, thanks to a small window and the street lights outside it, but the rays didn't extend to the open suite.

This was obviously Milo's backup. Or maybe it was his boss, Z.

That got Russ's heart pumping, but not just because he might finally come face-to-face with the baby seller, but because he didn't like two guns aimed anywhere near Julia.

Somehow, he had to get her out of this situation. Unfortunately, now that he was outgunned, he might need a miracle for that to happen.

"There's been a change of plans," Milo said. Minutes earlier, his nerves had started to show, but, he seemed back in control now.

Russ couldn't say the same for Julia. Her eyes were wide, and her breath was gusting.

"Just hang on," he whispered to her. She was stronger than she thought and could get through this, but he hated that she'd been put in this position again.

"What change of plans?" Russ asked Milo. Though he was pretty sure he already knew the answer. Milo only wanted one thing—the money.

"You give us the complete account number, and I'll let Julia live."

Russ looked him straight in the eye and knew that Milo was lying. Once he had the money, that would be it.

"For now though, I'll just make a few cuts," Milo continued. He kept the gun pointed at Julia, but used his left hand to take something from his pocket.

A switchblade.

Milo clicked it open, and the gleaming silver blade snapped up and caught the light. "I read all about Julia's attack, and I figured she'd have a particular distaste for knives. I'll keep cutting her until you drop the gun."

Hell!

Without the gun, Russ would have no way to protect Julia or himself. But he couldn't stand there and let Milo cut her to pieces, either.

Julia had her eyes fixed on the blade. She didn't struggle. She froze. Unable to break free without risking Russ's and her lives, she could no doubt see what was coming next.

This was the return of her worst nightmare.

Russ knew she wouldn't be able to handle this for long. Neither would he. He couldn't stand what this was doing to her. Even though he had no idea how to stop this, Russ did the only thing he could.

He dropped his gun.

Julia's gaze met his, and he saw the momentary relief when Milo pulled back the knife. But it was only momentary. Because like Russ, she knew that without the gun, they were in deep trouble.

"He'll have the account number on him," Milo told the person inside the room.

And then the person in the dark room stepped out.

Russ realized why he hadn't been able to make out any of the person's features. That's because Milo's henchman was dressed head-to-toe in all black, and that included a mesh cover over the face.

"Search him," Milo ordered.

The mysterious person checked Russ's pockets. Russ considered just grabbing the SOB and using him as a shield, the way Milo was using Julia. But there was a huge difference in their situations. Milo probably wouldn't care if Russ killed his accomplice.

Russ didn't want Julia harmed.

She was the ultimate bargaining tool, and Milo knew it.

Russ cursed. He'd been here before, with someone he cared about who was in danger, and it hadn't turned out so well the last time.

"It's not in his pockets?" Milo snapped.

His assistant shook his head.

Now, it was Milo who cursed. "Don't make me take out the knife again," Milo said to Russ. "Where's the account number?"

Russ debated what he should do, and finally said, "It's in the suite on the bar."

It was a huge risk, because he still wasn't sure if he could trust Silas, but maybe if Russ could split up these two goons, then he might be able to wrestle the gun away from Milo.

Milo tipped his head to his partner, and the person headed back to Julia's suite. Even in the dark, it wouldn't take long to see the white piece of paper that Russ had put amid the packs of nuts. He had a minute, maybe two, at the most.

Russ kept his attention fastened on Milo. And he counted down the seconds. Milo finally did what Russ had been waiting for him to do.

Milo glanced behind him at Julia's suite.

It was just a glance, a fraction of a second, but it was more than enough.

"Get down!" Russ shouted to Julia.

But he didn't wait for her to do that. Knowing he had only one shot at this, Russ dove right at Milo.

Chapter Seventeen

Julia didn't have time to get down before Russ launched himself at Milo. Russ plowed right into them, and all three of them went to the floor. Julia hit hard, nearly knocking the breath out of her, but she still tried to do whatever she could to help.

She rammed her arm against Milo to put some distance between them. It worked, even though Milo latched onto her hair and didn't let go.

Russ didn't let go of Milo either. He bashed his forehead against Milo's, and in the same motion Russ knocked the gun from Milo's hand.

The gun went flying across the hall and landed on the carpet.

Julia tried to go after it, but Milo wouldn't let go of her hair. He pulled hard, dragging her back toward him. The pain was excruciating, but she didn't scream. She concentrated all her energy on one thing: getting to that gun.

She couldn't let Milo or his partner get to it first because they would almost certainly use it on Russ and her. Russ continued to pound at Milo, trying to break the fierce grip he had on her.

Julia sensed some movement behind them, and she

glanced back to see Milo's partner. The sounds of the struggle had obviously made it into the suite, and the man had come running to help.

That couldn't happen. Because, unlike Milo, his hired gun was still in control of a weapon. Gathering as much strength as she could, Julia swung her body around so she could kick the gunman. She managed to connect with the person's shin, but the impact didn't dislodge his weapon.

Worse, he pointed the gun at Julia.

Julia had no doubt he would kill her on the spot, so she took drastic action. She dove back into the fracas with Russ and Milo. She barely dodged getting smacked in the head with Russ's fist. The blow hit Milo instead, but that didn't stop him from curving his arm around her neck.

Milo put her in a choke hold.

"I'll kill her!" Milo yelled to Russ.

Russ's answer was another fist to the man's face.

Julia fought with Milo's grip, and she fought to breathe. She couldn't let him win this. Nor could she let his hired gun get in a position to take a clean shot at Russ and her. As long as the three of them were wound around each other and fighting, the hired gun would have to wait to get a clear shot.

"Shoot them!" Milo told his comrade.

Julia didn't brace herself for the gunfire. She glanced back at the gunman, but she focused her energy on helping Russ get control of Milo. She bit and kicked and hit, all while trying to keep Milo between Russ and her.

The gunman waved his weapon, aiming and reaiming, obviously trying to take a shot that wouldn't hit Milo.

Without warning, Milo let go of her, and Julia fell backward, landing several feet away from Russ and Milo. She tried to scramble back into position so Milo's body would shield her, but it was too late.

The gunman fired.

The bullet came through a silencer, so there was no loud blast. Just the deadly swishing sound that Julia had heard when this latest attack began. The bullet didn't hit her, she realized. It slammed into the wall next to her. But it created just enough distraction for Russ to look her way.

"Julia!" Russ called out, as if pleading with her to get out of the line of fire.

And she tried to do that. She scrambled to the side so she could retrieve Milo's gun. However, the next shot was just the distraction Milo needed, because he latched onto her again and shoved her right in front of him.

"Move and she dies," Milo warned Russ.

Since the gunman was pointing his weapon at her and was less than three feet away, Julia didn't think she had much of a chance of dodging a bullet. The last time she'd gotten lucky, but she didn't think anyone could miss at this short range.

She went still—and waited.

Russ stopped struggling, as well, and they all looked at each other, as if trying to decide what to do next. The only sounds were their rough breaths.

With the quiet closing in around them and the gun pointed at her, Julia felt the old fears return. She wondered if she'd ever get to see Emily or Russ again.

Was this how it would all end?

But then she saw something that pushed away her thoughts of panic and death. She stared at the gunman dressed all in black. He even had on black gloves. And wore a net mask that curtained down from the black baseball cap.

There was something familiar about him.

Not so much anything visual about the person, but Julia caught the scent in the air. The scent that was cutting right though the sweat and humidity.

The scent was perfume.

Since she wasn't wearing any, that probably meant Milo's hired gun was a woman.

Was it Sylvia?

Julia wouldn't be surprised. The woman had tried to convince them she wanted to help by showing them those photographs, but Julia hadn't trusted her then. And she didn't trust her now.

"I know who you are," Julia told her.

The woman went stiff, and even though Julia couldn't see her eyes, she knew she was staring at her.

"Just kill her," Milo snarled. "Hell, what are you waiting for?"

But Russ didn't wait. He came off the floor and dove at the woman, crashing into her before she could get off a shot.

Julia didn't wait either. She went after Milo's gun. Unfortunately, Milo had the same idea. She barely managed to touch the weapon, when Milo jerked her away from it. He didn't stop there. Milo caught onto her and flung her against the wall.

Julia didn't have enough time to better position her body to take the impact, so her head slammed against a framed picture that'd been hung at eye level. She didn't even catch her breath before Milo came at her again.

She fought, punching at him and using her feet to keep him away. Next to her, just inches away, Russ was having his own battle, but she couldn't tell what was going on, because of the poor lighting and the way Milo was tossing her around like a rag doll.

"Run, Julia!" Russ told her.

She tried—she tried hard. But Milo just wouldn't let go.

From the corner of her eye, she saw Russ grab the woman and put the gun to her neck. He had control of the accomplice, but unless Julia could get away from Milo, the advantage would do them no good.

"I'll break her neck," Milo threatened. And he tightened his hands around her throat.

"Stop or I'll shoot," Russ threatened, right back. He jammed the gun against the woman and gave her hat and face covering a fierce jerk to remove it.

Julia froze, because it wasn't Sylvia. It was Tracy Richardson.

Maybe because she was no longer struggling, Milo stopped, too, and he looked back at Russ and Tracy.

"You should have shot them when you had the chance," Milo told her.

"Easy for you to say." Tracy didn't look nearly as composed as Milo. Her eyes were wild, and it was clear she was way out of her league here. "You're a killer. I'm not."

"What exactly are you?" Julia asked, hearing the anger in her own voice.

Tracy just gave an indignant stare.

"Tell them," Milo taunted. "If I'm the killer, then

you're a mother who arranged to have her own baby kidnapped. She's also the idiot who hired someone to fire shots at Julia and you in the park. And because that wasn't enough screwing up for one person, she hired the other moron to break into your suite."

"Why?" Russ wanted to know.

Milo didn't seem to mind telling all. "Because she got scared. I had the meeting all set up for tomorrow, and she decided she couldn't wait a few more hours. Amateur," he added, in a mumble.

Russ cursed, and if Julia hadn't gotten her teeth un-clenched, she might have done the same. "You had your baby stolen?" Julia wanted to know.

Tracy gave an indignant nod. "So what if I did."

That didn't help the anger that was slowly building into a rage inside Julia. "You put him in danger."

"He was never in danger. Not really."

That wasn't true. Any association with Milo was a dangerous one, and Tracy had put her son right in the line of fire. She'd apparently done the same to Russ and Julia, since Tracy hadn't denied it when Milo had accused her of hiring a hit man to fire those shots in the park.

"You did this for the money," Russ mumbled, his tone as enraged as Julia's.

"For *my* money," Tracy snapped. "I deserved it after putting up with Aaron's affairs for seven years. *Seven years!* But I was young and stupid when I married, and I signed a pre-nup. I wouldn't have gotten a penny in the divorce, so this was my way of making sure my son and I had a good future."

"It was your way of staying rich," Julia corrected.

Tracy glared at her. "I don't have to take this from

you. Break her neck, Milo. Agent Gentry won't kill an unarmed woman."

"The hell I won't." Russ jammed the gun to her face.

"Stop!" Milo yelled. "Even with Tracy's impatience and penchant for messing everything up, we can all get what we want here. I need the numbers for that offshore account, and you two can still get to rescue the baby. Everyone lives, and the only one who's out anything is Aaron Richardson."

None of that soothed Julia's anger. She wanted both of these monsters to pay for what they'd done.

"What about the hurt agent on the floor?" Russ asked. "What about your own hired guns? Two people are dead, Milo."

"All Tracy's fault. The agent on the floor had been drugged. You can thank her for that, too. None of this, including the hired guns, can be traced back to me. She knows, if this all goes wrong she'll take the blame. I'll just walk away."

Tracy mumbled something under her breath. She obviously wasn't happy that Milo was ready to throw her under a bus. What could she have expected? She was dealing with a hard-core criminal.

Julia glanced down at her hands. She wasn't shaking. And she wasn't on the verge of a panic attack. But she hated that Russ and she were still in danger, and it might not end anytime soon. One thing was for sure. She didn't intend to stay in Milo's grip.

She drew back her elbow and rammed it into his stomach. In the same motion, she bolted forward and snatched up the gun from the floor. It took everything in her to stop herself from firing at the man who'd made their lives a living hell, and had sent Emily into hiding.

"You know where the Richardson baby is?" Russ asked, tipping his head to Milo.

"I do. He's…nearby. Why?"

"Because I'll make a deal with you. Who's Z?"

She couldn't see Milo's expression, but she thought he might have smiled. "I am. Z is the name I give to the sellers who get in touch with me. Most people respond better if they think they're dealing with a team, rather than an individual."

Well, that was one riddle solved.

"Mind you, that's not a confession to any crime," Milo explained. "People just seem to think the worst of me, and assume I can find them buyers for the children they've acquired through illegal means."

"Can't imagine why," Russ snarled. "So, here's what we'll do. First, you put that knife on the floor."

Milo hesitated, as if giving that some thought, but he finally took it from his pocket, and tossed it so that it landed near Julia's feet. She tried not to react, but she couldn't suppress a shiver. She kicked the switchblade to the side.

"I'll give you the offshore account numbers, and you give me the baby," Russ told Milo. "I'll let you walk. Tracy here, however, will get to spend the rest of her life in prison."

"What?" Tracy yelled.

Milo seemed to relax. "Sounds like a good deal to me. Let's start for the parking lot, while you give me the first half of the account number."

"This isn't going to happen," Tracy shouted.

"You're wrong," Russ informed her. He shoved her, to get her moving.

They began walking. Not quickly, and Tracy didn't exactly break any speed records. She loped along, all the while cursing her former partner.

All of them continued to fire glances at each other. Since Russ kept his gun aimed at Tracy, Julia concentrated on Milo. She wasn't even sure she could shoot straight, but if the man made one wrong move, she would stop him.

"Six, four, eight, eight, three," Russ said, but Julia had no idea if that was a correct set of numbers or not.

While they continued to make their way down the hall, Milo reached for his phone, causing Russ to aim the gun at him.

"It's just my cell. I want to verify that there is indeed an account that starts with those numbers."

Russ hesitated a moment, then motioned for him to continue. That brought a sound of outrage from Tracy.

"I can't believe you're letting him do this." Tracy stopped, but Russ just ground the gun against her and shoved her forward.

Milo led them to the stairs, and Julia was thankful for the emergency lighting. She could actually see the steps, and she could also see that no one was lurking there, ready to ambush them.

"Confirmed," Milo said, a moment later. He held onto his phone, probably so he'd have quick access when and if Russ gave him the other numbers.

"Open the door," Russ instructed Milo, when they reached the exit. "And Julia, you stay behind him. Shoot him if he does anything that makes you uncomfortable."

She nodded and made brief eye contact with Russ, to see how he was doing. He had his attention on the task. Good thing, too. She didn't want his concern for her to cause him to lose focus.

The moment Milo opened the door, the heat and humidity rushed in and engulfed them. It was night, but the parking lot was actually better lit than the hotel. And there was the sound of sirens. Finally, the police were responding. The problem was, they might see the guns and start firing. That meant Russ and she had to move fast.

"The baby's in one of the vehicles," Milo insisted.

Julia looked around at the half-dozen cars parked in the back lot.

"Which one?" Russ demanded.

Milo shook his head.

"I'll look in all of them," Julia volunteered.

"If you do that, the nanny has instructions to drive away," Milo explained. "The only way she'll stay put is if I tell her, with a call."

"Nine, four, three," Russ said, giving Milo more of the numbers.

"Don't do this!" Tracy yelled. She was crying now, the tears streaming down her cheeks, and she sounded beyond hysterical. "Make the deal with me. Not him. That's my baby. All Milo wants is the money."

The men ignored her, and Milo looked at Julia. "Start walking to that dark blue van at the back of the parking lot."

"It's not the blue van," Tracy insisted. "It's the white

car." She glared at Milo. "I'll be damned if I let you take my money and stick me in jail."

"She's lying," Milo insisted.

"I don't think so," Russ mumbled, and Julia agreed. "Why don't we all have a look?"

Russ used his gun to get Milo and Tracy walking in the direction of the white car. Julia held her breath, hoping Milo was wrong about the driver taking off if she didn't get the phone call.

"Keep Milo in front of you, Julia," Russ instructed. She did, even though she prayed shooting him wouldn't be necessary. Julia didn't want shots fired with the baby around.

She approached the car.

And she saw the driver. It was a young woman with a death grip on the steering wheel. She was obviously terrified. Then Julia saw something else.

There was a sleeping baby in a carrier on the back-seat.

"That's the Richardson boy," Russ confirmed, probably because he'd seen photos in his investigation.

Julia opened the car door and motioned for the nanny-driver to get out. She did, and the woman began to rattle off something in Spanish while she cried uncontrollably. Julia reached for the keys to take them out of the ignition. Her back was turned for just a second when she heard the sound.

She whirled around, gun and keys in hand, and saw Milo dive toward Russ. Her heart dropped. *No, this couldn't happen.* They were so close to bringing this to an end.

Tracy managed to get out of the way, but Russ took the full impact of Milo's body crashing into his. Both men went to the pavement, and Russ's gun flew out of his hand.

The fight began all over again, fists flying, their bodies twisting around, so that it made it impossible for Julia to take aim. She couldn't risk shooting Russ, or having a bullet ricochet and hit the baby.

The nanny started to run, but Julia didn't go after her. She had to stay and try to help Russ.

Milo delivered a hard punch to Russ's jaw, but it didn't seem to faze him. However, Julia felt it, it seemed as if the pain shot through her.

Russ was operating on pure, raw adrenaline and had no fear of dying or being beaten. Julia had enough fear for both of them. She didn't want either of them to die before she'd had a chance to tell him that she was in love with him.

"Don't," Julia warned Tracy, when the woman started after the gun.

Tracy stopped. Thank God. Julia didn't want to risk firing a shot at her, either.

Russ brought back his fist and slammed it into Milo's face.

"But I have to leave," Tracy begged, glancing back at the struggle that was about to end. "As a mother, you must understand. If I go to jail, I won't be able to see my baby."

Julia looked her straight in the eyes. "You don't deserve to see him."

Tracy's face tightened and she let out a feral howl. She came at Julia and pushed her away from the car. Julia still couldn't fire, for fear of hitting Russ or the baby. But she also had no intentions of letting Tracy get anywhere near the son she'd had stolen for money.

Julia put all of her anger and emotions into the hard grip she had on Tracy's shoulder. She slammed the woman against the car and pinned her there.

"If I have to, I will kill you," Julia warned her.

Tracy stared at her, and Julia could see the debate in her eyes. It didn't last long. Tracy went limp and started to sob again.

Julia didn't take the gun off the woman, but she took her eyes off her just for a second so she could check on Russ.

Just a second.

She saw the gun, not in Russ's hand, but in Milo's.

And then the shot rang out.

Chapter Eighteen

Everything seemed to freeze.

One moment Milo and Russ were in a fight to gain control of the gun. The next moment, Russ heard the shot. He looked around and tried to figure out what had happened. And in those moments, he had a horrible thought: that the bullet had hit Julia.

He heard her scream, except it wasn't a scream, exactly. She was calling out his name. Her voice was filled with panic, and it merged with the piercing sounds of the sirens and the frantic shouts from the police who were approaching the scene.

Russ felt the gun that was between him and Milo. Both of them had their hands gripped around it.

It was Milo's finger on the trigger.

Hell, has Milo shot me? Russ wondered.

Russ looked at the man whose face was only a few inches from his own. Everything still felt frozen, except for Julia's screams. He had to check on her. He had to make sure she was all right, but he couldn't move, because Milo's weight was pinning him in place.

Dead weight.

Russ saw his lifeless eyes, then he looked between their bodies. Milo had indeed pulled the trigger, but the gun had been aimed at his own chest. He'd killed himself.

Russ was betting that it was an accident, because men like Milo didn't commit suicide.

"I'm all right," Russ tried to tell Julia, but he wasn't sure she heard him.

He threw Milo off him, and in case this attack wasn't over, he wrenched the gun from the dead man's hand.

Julia came racing toward him but stopped a few feet away. She had no color in her face, and she stared at him with her fingers pressed to her mouth.

"I'm okay," Russ said again.

But she shook her head and pointed to his chest.

Russ looked down, wondering if he had been shot after all, and he saw the blood. Now he understood.

"It's Milo's, not mine," he told her. He got to his feet and went to her as quickly as he could. He pulled her into his arms.

"Milo's," she mumbled. "Not yours. You're alive."

"Yeah." But it was obvious that Julia was about to fall apart. He didn't blame her. She'd been through hell and back tonight.

Behind them, Tracy latched onto the car door as if she were going to open it. "Don't," Russ warned her, and he pointed his gun at her. "It's over."

He had to let go of Julia so he could get a better aim and remove his badge from his back pocket. From the corner of his eye, he saw the uniformed officers approach the scene. Silas and Toby were with them, and Silas was being helped into an ambulance.

Later, he would apologize to Silas for not trusting him. But for now, he needed to get the Richardson baby out of here and tend to Julia.

Russ lifted his badge so the officers could see it. "Special Agent Russ Gentry," he let them know.

"I love you," Julia blurted out.

Even though there was pure chaos going on around them, that still grabbed every bit of Russ's attention. "Excuse me?" Because he was sure he'd misheard her.

"I love you." She gave a shaky, confirming nod. "I wanted you to know."

It was hardly the appropriate time, but Russ kissed her—and then eased her away from him. "Hold that thought," he whispered.

Russ went to Toby, who was barking out orders to the uniformed officers. Thankfully, he'd filled them in on what was happening, because one of the cops rushed to take Tracy Richardson into custody. The woman continued to sob, and she pled for a deal.

"The baby's father is on the way," Toby let Russ know. "Sorry I was late getting here. I was at the police station, questioning Sylvia."

"Sylvia? What did she have to say?"

"A lot. Apparently, she learned the love of her life, Milo, had been sleeping with Tracy Richardson. That didn't sit well with her, so she's spilling her guts."

Good. That might insure that Tracy would receive

a maximum sentence. As for Milo, well, he'd already gotten what he deserved.

"I didn't know what was going on here at the hotel, until I heard on the monitor that the local police were responding to sounds of gunshots," Toby added.

"I think Milo jammed the phone lines and cut the power," Russ said, nodding his head toward the lifeless man. One of the uniforms was checking him out.

Despite the fact that his full attention should be on what was happening, Russ's gaze went back to Julia. She'd opened the back door of the car and was trying to comfort the baby. Obviously, the shouts and the gunfire had woken him, and he was crying at the top of his lungs.

"Is Julia okay?" Toby asked.

"I think so." *Well…except that she'd just told me that she loved me.*

Had that been the adrenaline talking?

It made him a little sick to think that it might have been. Russ wasn't exactly surprised that he wanted it to be real. He'd wanted a lot of things from Julia, from the first moment he'd laid eyes on her.

First, he'd wanted sex. Then, more. The question was—how much more?

"I found Silas staggering out the front door of the hotel," Toby continued. "He'd been drugged, but was able to tell me some of what was going on. He said Tracy had him kidnapped so he'd look guilty." It'd worked.

"How is he?"

"He'll be fine. He has a broken arm and he's dehydrated, but I'm sure the medics will fix him up."

So that was one less thing on Russ's plate to worry about. Of course, there were still gaps he needed to fill in.

"There's a dead gunman on the floor of Julia's suite. According to Milo, Tracy hired him because she knew I was a federal agent. She also hired the other gunman in the park."

Toby nodded. "She obviously wanted you out of the way, and maybe Julia, too. She probably thought you were getting too close to figuring out that she's the one who had her son stolen."

"Can you make a call?" Russ asked Toby. "I think it'd help Julia and me if Emily were on her way back to us."

Toby studied him, probably because there was way too much emotion in his voice, but the agent finally nodded. "I'll get right on that. It'll be the first call I make." And the agent proceeded to do just that.

Russ took a deep breath and looked back at Julia. She had the baby in her arms and was rocking him back and forth, trying to soothe him. Russ had faced down gunmen recently, but he hadn't been this nervous.

But then, he'd never had this much at stake.

Once Toby had made the call, Russ finished up the briefing. He needed to give the agent some of the details of what had happened, so the reports could get started. Tracy would need to be interrogated as well. The nanny who'd run from the car would have to be found. Sylvia would have to be questioned further, so the FBI could determine what exactly she knew about Milo's baby-selling activities.

So many details. However, Russ was going to leave those details to someone else.

After he'd finished with Toby, Russ made his way across the parking lot toward Julia. She looked up, snared his gaze. He thought for a moment that she might smile, but then her attention dropped to his shirt.

Specifically, to the blood.

"How's the baby?" he asked, to give himself time to gather his thoughts.

"He's okay. Not a scratch." As if he knew he was now the topic of discussion, the baby stopped crying and volleyed glances at them. "His mother will go to jail, but he still has his father."

Yeah. That was more than Emily had. But then, Emily had Julia and him.

"Come on," Russ said, taking her by the arm. "Let's go in the hotel lobby."

He didn't want her to have to keep looking at Milo's body—and his bloody shirt. He stripped it off and gave it to one of the agents who was at the back entrance of the hotel.

"You should probably bag this," Russ told him. It almost certainly wouldn't be needed, but he wanted it out of Julia's sight. Besides, Emily would arrive soon, and he didn't want the baby around it, either.

The agent was wearing a button-down shirt over a tee, so he took off the outer shirt and handed it to Russ. Russ thanked him and put it on.

Julia gave a nod of approval. "I'm glad Milo's dead," she whispered. "If he'd gotten away—"

"He didn't," Russ reminded her. "And neither did Tracy. It's all over, Julia. We're safe now."

She gave another shaky nod, and even though she didn't seem ready to panic, Russ was still worried about her. Even more, he was worried about how to say the things he needed to say.

They took their time walking inside, probably because Julia was drained, and seemed to pause with each step. Russ felt the fatigue, too, but more than that, he felt relief that they'd all come through this unscathed.

When the baby started to fuss again, Julia placed him against her chest and patted his back. A female uniformed officer stepped forward. "Want me to take him? His father just arrived."

Julia kissed the little boy on the cheek and handed him over. The officer had no sooner taken the baby when Russ spotted Aaron Richardson coming in through the front lobby doors. No slow steps for him. The man practically ran to his son, and gathered him into his arms.

If Russ had any doubts about Aaron's love for his son, he didn't have them after witnessing that encounter.

"Thank you," Aaron told them, and he just kept repeating it while he kissed his baby. The man started to cry.

Several officers and an agent converged on Aaron, probably to fill him in on the details of what had happened to his wife. Russ decided those were not details

Julia needed to relive, so he led her into the reception area and had her sit on one of the sofas with him.

"It's okay," she reassured him. "I'm not about to fall apart."

He examined her face and realized that it was true. She was shaky of course, but it would have been unnatural if she hadn't been.

She examined his face, too, and nibbled on her bottom lip. "About what I said in the parking lot—"

"You can't take it back," Russ said, interrupting her.

Julia stopped nibbling and stared at him. "I don't want to take it back."

"Really?"

"Really," she assured him. "I just wanted to apologize for blurting it out there, when you had so much else on your mind."

That eased the knot in his stomach, but he knew something else would ease it more. Russ put his hand around the back of her neck and drew her to him for a kiss. Not a quick peck of reassurance. He put his heart and soul into this one.

When he pulled back, Julia made a silky sigh. "Good," she whispered.

Yes, it was; but he wanted better. He wanted *more*.

"I'm in love with you, too," he told her.

Julia's eyes widened and she froze. For one terrifying moment, Russ thought she was about to say that she didn't want him to be in love with her, that it wouldn't work out between them, but a smile curved her beautiful mouth.

"Are you just saying that because we nearly died?" she asked, cautiously.

"No. I'm saying that because it's true."

She seemed to be holding her breath. "You're sure?"

"A million percent. I don't need months or years to sort out my feelings for you. I love you, plain and simple. And I love Emily, too. I want us to adopt her—together. I want her to have the Gentry name, because I think that would have pleased R.J. and Lissa."

Tears filled her eyes, but since she was still smiling, Russ thought this was better. He gathered his breath, and his courage, and he went in for the big prize.

"Marry me?" Russ asked.

"Can we get married?" Julia said at the same moment.

Both of them stared at each other. And despite the investigation going on around them, they laughed.

They were still laughing when the lobby doors swung open and in came Agent Soto, Zoey and Emily.

Russ and Julia jumped up from the sofa and hurried toward the baby. Russ got there first, but he stepped back so that Julia could scoop Emily into her arms.

The baby was sleeping, but she lifted one eye to check out what was happening. Emily must not have deemed this big enough to warrant waking up from her nap.

Julia kissed the baby and passed her to Russ. The gesture felt as natural as anything he'd ever experienced. This was right, and he knew exactly what he had to do to make the rightness stay that way.

"Could you excuse us a minute?" Russ asked Zoey and Soto. With Emily still cradled in his arm, he led

Julia back into the reception area. "I believe we owe each other an answer. I asked you to marry me, and you did the same."

He paused a heartbeat.

"The answer is yes," they said together.

The energy between them seemed electric, as it always did when they were together. It was even more special because Emily was there.

Russ put his arm around Julia and stole another kiss. He made it long, hot and special—because it was the first kiss of their new life together with their daughter, Emily.

* * * * *

*As the effects of the hostage situation continue
to change lives, be sure to pick up
the next installment in Delores Fossen's*
Texas Maternity: Hostages *miniseries
coming in July 2010.
Look for THE MOMMY MYSTERY
wherever Harlequin Intrigue books are sold!*

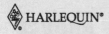
HARLEQUIN®

INTRIGUE

COMING NEXT MONTH

Available July 13, 2010

REQUEST YOUR FREE BOOKS!

2 FREE NOVELS
PLUS 2
FREE GIFTS!

 HARLEQUIN®
INTRIGUE®

Breathtaking Romantic Suspense

YES! Please send me 2 FREE Harlequin Intrigue® novels and my 2 FREE gifts (gifts are worth about $10). After receiving them, if I don't wish to receive any more books, I can return the shipping statement marked "cancel." If I don't cancel, I will receive 6 brand-new novels every month and be billed just $4.24 per book in the U.S. or $4.99 per book in Canada. That's a saving of at least 15% off the cover price! It's quite a bargain! Shipping and handling is just 50¢ per book.* I understand that accepting the 2 free books and gifts places me under no obligation to buy anything. I can always return a shipment and cancel at any time. Even if I never buy another book from Harlequin, the two free books and gifts are mine to keep forever.

182/382 HDN E5MG

Name _____ (PLEASE PRINT) _____

Address _____ Apt. #

City _____ State/Prov. _____ Zip/Postal Code

Signature (if under 18, a parent or guardian must sign)

Mail to the **Harlequin Reader Service:**
IN U.S.A.: P.O. Box 1867, Buffalo, NY 14240-1867
IN CANADA: P.O. Box 609, Fort Erie, Ontario L2A 5X3
Not valid for current subscribers to Harlequin Intrigue books.

**Are you a subscriber to Harlequin Intrigue books and
want to receive the larger-print edition? Call 1-800-873-8635 today!**

* Terms and prices subject to change without notice. Prices do not include applicable taxes. N.Y. residents add applicable sales tax. Canadian residents will be charged applicable provincial taxes and GST. Offer not valid in Quebec. This offer is limited to one order per household. All orders subject to approval. Credit or debit balances in a customer's account(s) may be offset by any other outstanding balance owed by or to the customer. Please allow 4 to 6 weeks for delivery. Offer available while quantities last.

Your Privacy: Harlequin is committed to protecting your privacy. Our Privacy Policy is available online at www.eHarlequin.com or upon request from the Reader Service. From time to time we make our lists of customers available to reputable third parties who may have a product or service of interest to you. If you would prefer we not share your name and address, please check here. ☐

Help us get it right—We strive for accurate, respectful and relevant communications. To clarify or modify your communication preferences, visit us at www.ReaderService.com/consumerschoice.

HI10R

HARLEQUIN®

A Romance

FOR EVERY MOOD™

Spotlight on

Heart & Home

Heartwarming romances
where love can happen
right when you least expect it.

See the next page to enjoy a sneak peek
from Silhouette Special Edition®,
a Heart and Home series.

CATHHSSE10

Introducing McFARLANE'S PERFECT BRIDE
by USA TODAY bestselling author Christine Rimmer,
from Silhouette Special Edition®.

Entranced. Captivated. Enchanted.

Connor sat across the table from Tori Jones and couldn't help thinking that those words exactly described what effect the small-town schoolteacher had on him. He might as well stop trying to tell himself he wasn't interested. He was powerfully drawn to her.

Clearly, he should have dated more when he was younger.

There had been a couple of other women since Jennifer had walked out on him. But he had never been entranced. Or captivated. Or enchanted.

Until now.

He wanted her—*her,* Tori Jones, in particular. Not just someone suitably attractive and well-bred, as Jennifer had been. Not just someone sophisticated, sexually exciting and discreet, which pretty much described the two women he'd dated after his marriage crashed and burned.

It came to him that he…he *liked* this woman. And that was new to him. He liked her quick wit, her wisdom and her big heart. He liked the passion in her voice when she talked about things she believed in.

He liked *her.* And suddenly it mattered all out of proportion that she might like him, too.

Was he losing it? He couldn't help but wonder. Was he cracking under the strain—of the soured economy, the McFarlane House setbacks, his divorce, the scary changes in his son? Of the changes he'd decided he needed to make in his life and himself?

Strangely, right then, on his first date with Tori Jones, he didn't care if he just might be going over the edge. He was having a great time—having *fun*, of all things—and he didn't want it to end.

Is Connor finally able to admit his feelings to Tori, and are they reciprocated?
Find out in McFARLANE'S PERFECT BRIDE
by USA TODAY bestselling author Christine Rimmer.
Available July 2010,
only from Silhouette Special Edition®.

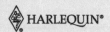

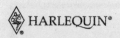
HARLEQUIN®

Showcase

LESLIE KELLY
Naturally Naughty

Wicked & Willing

On sale June 8

Reader favorites from the most talented voices in romance

Save $1.00 on the purchase of 1 or more Harlequin® Showcase books.

SAVE $1.00 on the purchase of 1 or more Harlequin® Showcase books.

Coupon expires November 30, 2010. Redeemable at participating retail outlets.
Limit one coupon per customer. Valid in the U.S.A. and Canada only.

52609057

Canadian Retailers: Harlequin Enterprises Limited will pay the face value of this coupon plus 10.25¢ if submitted by customer for this product only. Any other use constitutes fraud. Coupon is nonassignable. Void if taxed, prohibited or restricted by law. Consumer must pay any government taxes. Void if copied. Nielsen Clearing House ("NCH") customers submit coupons and proof of sales to Harlequin Enterprises Limited, P.O. Box 3000, Saint John, NB E2L 4L3, Canada. Non-NCH retailer—for reimbursement submit coupons and proof of sales directly to Harlequin Enterprises Limited, Retail Marketing Department, 225 Duncan Mill Rd., Don Mills, ON M3B 3K9, Canada.

5 65373 00076 2   (8100)0 11654

U.S. Retailers: Harlequin Enterprises Limited will pay the face value of this coupon plus 8¢ if submitted by customer for this product only. Any other use constitutes fraud. Coupon is nonassignable. Void if taxed, prohibited or restricted by law. Consumer must pay any government taxes. Void if copied. For reimbursement submit coupons and proof of sales directly to Harlequin Enterprises Limited, P.O. Box 880478, El Paso, TX 88588-0478, U.S.A. Cash value 1/100 cents.

® and TM are trademarks owned and used by the trademark owner and/or its licensee.
© 2010 Harlequin Enterprises Limited

HSCCOUP0610